# A PIG CALLED LOLLIPOP

First published individually as
*Lady Lollipop* (2000), and *Clever Lollipop* (2003)
by Walker Books Ltd, 87 Vauxhall Walk, London SE11 5HJ

This edition published 2022

2 4 6 8 10 9 7 5 3 1

Text © 2000, 2003 Fox Busters Ltd
Cover Illustration and Inside Illustrations © 2022 Anna Chernyshova

The right of Dick King-Smith and Anna Chernyshova to be identified
as author and illustrator respectively of this work has been asserted in
accordance with the Copyright, Designs and Patents Act 1988

This book has been typeset in Stempel Schneidler and
Jacobs Rubberstamp

Printed and bound by CPI Group (UK) Ltd, Croydon CR0 4YY

British Library Cataloguing in Publication Data:
a catalogue record for this book is
available from the British Library

ISBN 978-1-5295-0465-1

www.walker.co.uk
www.dickkingsmith.com

# DICK KING-SMITH

# A PIG CALLED LOLLIPOP

illustrated by Anna Chernyshova

**WALKER BOOKS**

# Lady Lollipop

7

# Clever Lollipop

*99*

# LADY
# LOLLIPOP

# CONTENTS

CHAPTER ONE ~ *10*
*Was there ever such a
spoiled child?*

CHAPTER TWO ~ *15*
*"A bit of a strange name"*

CHAPTER THREE ~ *24*
*"I wonder if I could train her?"*

CHAPTER FOUR ~ *32*
*"Busy! Understand?"*

CHAPTER FIVE ~ *38*
*"I'll jolly well make
you a duke"*

CHAPTER SIX ~ *45*
*"You always want to
get your own way"*

CHAPTER SEVEN ~ 52
*"What a good girl!"*

CHAPTER EIGHT ~ 58
*"If the pig comes in,
Mummy goes out"*

CHAPTER NINE ~ 66
*"Wipe your feet"*

CHAPTER TEN ~ 75
*"She had better come
in to tea"*

CHAPTER ELEVEN ~ 86
*I'll give the boy a job*

CHAPTER TWELVE ~ 94
*"Lady Lollipop!"*

## *Was there ever such a spoiled child?*

Once upon a time, in a faraway land, there lived a little princess. She was seven years old, soon to be eight, with short brown hair and large brown eyes, and she was a very spoiled child.

Her mother, Queen Ethelwynne, spoiled her quite a bit, but her father, King Theophilus, spoiled her rotten.

So that all the courtiers at the Royal Palace, and all the servants too, from the Lord High Chamberlain to the smallest scullery boy, agreed among themselves that little Princess Penelope was a right pain in the neck.

As her eighth birthday approached, the King and Queen were discussing what they should buy their beloved only child as a present.

"What about a pony, Eth?" said the King.

"I don't think she likes horses very much, Theo," the Queen replied. "How about a puppy?"

"She's never been too keen on dogs," said the King.

"Well, a kitten then?"

"Or cats," said the King.

"Well then, let's ask her what she would like," said the Queen.

"But then it won't be a surprise. Still, I expect you're right. Let's have her in and see what she says."

So they sent a servant to summon the Princess, and waited.

And waited.

"She can have absolutely anything she likes, of course," said the King.

"Well, I don't know…" began the Queen.

"Absolutely anything," said the King.

Shortly the servant returned with a message from Princess Penelope that she would come when she was ready and not before.

King Theophilus laughed.

"She's got a will of her own, has our Penelope," he said.

"You can say that again," said the Queen.

Just then the door burst open and in came

the little Princess with a face like thunder.

"What d'you want?" she said. "You interrupted a game I was playing."

"Now, now," said the Queen, and "Steady on, old girl," said the King. "We want to ask you something. What would you like for a present on your eighth birthday? A pony?"

"Don't like horses," said the Princess.

"A puppy then?" asked the Queen.

"Don't like dogs."

"Or a kitten?"

"Or cats."

"Well, you tell us, darling," said King Theophilus. "What *would* you like?"

"A pig," said the Princess.

"What!"

"I want a pig for a pet."

"A pig, Penelope?" cried the Queen. "But a pig is a dirty animal."

"Is not!" said the Princess.

"A pig," said the King, "is an ugly beast."

"Is not!!" shouted the Princess.

"A pig," said the King and Queen with one voice, "is a stupid creature."

"Is not!!!" yelled the Princess at the top of her voice.

"I wanna pig, I wanna pig, I wanna pig!"

So loudly did she yell that everyone in the Royal Palace heard her, from the Lord High Chamberlain to the smallest scullery boy, and everyone thought, Was there ever such a spoiled child?

Queen Ethelwynne looked at her husband.

"'She can have absolutely anything.' That's what you said, Theo," she remarked.

King Theophilus sighed.

"All right then, my sweet," he said. "Daddy will buy you a pig."

## CHAPTER TWO

# "A bit of a strange name"

The first thing that the King did was to issue
a Royal Proclamation, which stated that every
pig-keeper in the kingdom was commanded to
bring one pig to the Palace at a certain time on
the day of Princess Penelope's eighth birthday.

"That way, Eth," said the King to the Queen, "our Penelope will have the widest possible choice."

So, when the time came, dozens and dozens of pig-keepers gathered in the Great Park, in the centre of which the Palace stood.

Each man had brought one pig, in a cart or on a rope or, if small enough, in his arms, and what a selection there was. There were big pigs and middle-sized pigs and little pigs, there were pigs with upright ears or droopy ears, with long snouts or pushed-in faces, and as for colour, why, there were pigs of every imaginable hue. Many were whitish of course, but some were black, some reddish, some stripy, some spotted, all lined up on the green grass of the Great Park, ready for the Princess's inspection.

Most of the pig-keepers knew that the Princess was a very spoiled child, and many of them expected that she would not be satisfied with just one pig. The King and the Queen rather expected this too, and they kept their fingers crossed as they walked along the lines behind the birthday girl.

But, far from choosing lots, the Princess passed from pig to pig and all she said was "No."

"Do you like this one, Penelope darling?" the King would say.

"No."

"Or this one perhaps," the Queen would say.

"No!"

But after a bit they gave up asking, because "No!" became "NO!!"

"I'll tell you when I find the one I want," said the little Princess. "Just stop nagging me."

Each pig-keeper was of course very disappointed as the inspection party passed him by, for to have had his pig chosen to live at Court would have been the greatest honour.

But it was beginning to look as though the Princess simply couldn't find anything she liked. Whatever the size or shape or colour, she merely scowled and shook her head and marched on.

Until there was only one animal left, at the very end of the very last of the lines of pigs of all sorts.

This last pig, the King and Queen could see, was quite different from all the other fat, well-groomed animals. They say that pig-keepers tend to look rather like their charges, and most of the owners were, if not well-groomed, on the fat side. But the last pig was a long skinny creature, held on the end of a piece of string by a long skinny boy. It was a dirty white in colour and the boy looked none too clean.

Princess Penelope pointed at this last pig.

"Want *that* one," she said.

"But darling," said the King, "you can't have that one. It's the scruffiest, ugliest pig of the lot."

"Is *not*!" shouted the Princess, and she folded her arms and scowled furiously at her father.

Now all the pig-keepers in the Great Park fell silent and so even did their pigs. Everyone waited to see who would win this battle – the King, monarch of all he surveyed, or his spoiled little daughter.

But before either could say a further word, to everyone's surprise, the last pig's owner spoke.

"You're right, miss," said the boy to the Princess. "You've picked the best one. Scruffy and ugly she may be, like your dad says, but she's the brightest, cleverest pig you ever did see. Just watch this."

Then he said to his pig "Sit" and she sat, and "Down" and she lay down, and "Roll over" and she rolled over, and "Stand" and she stood up again, looking up at the boy and waiting for the next command.

"Will you look at that!" said the other pig-keepers in astonishment, while their pigs voiced their amazement in a flurry of grunting.

"I trained her myself," said the long skinny boy, and he handed the end of the string to the Princess. He swallowed, as though there was a lump in his throat.

"I shall be ever so sorry to see her go," he said. "She's all I've got."

"You must have a mother and father, haven't you?" said the Queen.

"No, I'm an orphan."

"Oh well, don't worry," said Princess Penelope. "Daddy will get you another pig," and she took hold of the animal's string and said "Sit."

The pig remained standing.

The Princess stamped her foot.

"SIT!" she shouted again, but nothing happened.

"Choose another pig, Penelope, my love," said King Theophilus. "This creature only obeys the boy."

To everyone's surprise, the Princess did not shout and yell at this. Instead she stood, hands on hips, facing her father and said in a very quiet voice, "I … want … this … pig."

"Oh," said the King. "Sorry," he said to the boy, "she wants your one."

"Could I come and see her, now and again?" the boy said. "The pig, I mean?"

He turned to the Princess.

"Could I, miss, please?"

Now, as this oddly assorted couple of children faced one another – the Princess in a new, expensive party frock, the boy, half a head taller, in his torn and dirty clothes – something quite unexpected happened.

The Princess smiled.

Whether it was because she felt some pity for the boy, or whether she'd worked out that he'd be useful for jobs like mucking out the pig, or whether it was because the pig suddenly sat down before her and looked up into her eyes and gave a little grunt, no one knew. But those nearest saw her smiling, first at the pig and then at the ragged boy.

"What's your name?" she said.

"Johnny, miss. Johnny Skinner."

"All right, Johnny Skinner," said Princess Penelope. "You can be my personal pig-keeper. You can go on looking after this pig, which is now *my* pig, my birthday pig. Understood?"

"Yes, miss," said Johnny.

"But darling…" began the Queen.

"But Penelope…" began the King.

"But nothing," said the Princess. "Come on, Johnny."

And back they marched along the lines, the Princess with her birthday present, then Johnny Skinner, then King Theophilus and then Queen Ethelwynne.

"By the way," said the Princess over her shoulder to her new pig-keeper, "what's her name, this pig of mine?"

"Well, miss," said Johnny, "it's a bit of a strange name really, but it's what I've always called her."

"What is it?"

"Lollipop."

# *"I wonder if I could train her?"*

"I like it," said the Princess. "It's a nice name.
But why is she so thin? Don't you feed her
properly?"

"I've no money to buy food for her," said
Johnny Skinner.

"What's she been eating then?"

"Whatever she could find on the rubbish heaps, miss."

"We'll have to do something about that," said the Princess.

When they reached the Palace gates, she stopped and turned to face her father.

"Daddy," she said.

"Yes, darling?"

"I want…" and she went through a whole list of things she wanted done.

"Yes, certainly, my love," said the King.

So that by the end of the day, no one who had seen her that morning in the Great Park would have recognized the pig called Lollipop. She had been washed and scrubbed and groomed and oiled, and she lay in a deep bed of clean straw in one of the loose boxes in the Royal Mews, her stomach filled with a lovely mess of rich scraps from the Royal table and leftovers from the Royal kitchens.

By her side sat a very different-looking boy, for Johnny Skinner had taken a proper bath (for the first time in his life), and his old clothes had all been burned. Kitted out in new ones, his stomach also comfortably full, he got to his feet as the door of the loose box opened and in came Princess Penelope, carrying a birthday cake with eight candles on it.

"Here we are, Johnny," she said. "I had to give a bit each to Daddy and Mummy, but the rest is ours," and she cut three big slices.

"Thanks, miss," said Johnny, and Lollipop grunted.

Though the boy could not know it, a bit of a change had come over the birthday girl. Because of her rank and because of her spoiled and often sulky nature, she had never had any real friends. Now she was beginning to feel she had one.

"You shouldn't really call me 'miss', Johnny," she said.

"Why not, miss?"

"Because you should address me as 'Your Royal Highness'."

"Oh."

"But actually I don't mind. Have some more cake."

So he did, and she did, and so did the pig, till there was nothing left but the eight candles, and then Lollipop ate them too.

Princess Penelope stroked her pig.

"Sit," she said, but the pig remained standing.

The Princess pouted.

"Why won't she do what I tell her?" she said. "Everyone else does what I tell them, why won't my pig?"

"It's early days, miss," said Johnny. "She's only ever been used to me."

"Well, she's not yours any longer," said the Princess sharply, "and don't you forget it." And out she flounced.

"Don't you worry," said Johnny to Lollipop. "I shall always think of you as mine," and he rubbed the roots of her ears, something she specially liked, so that she gave little soft squeaks of pleasure.

"They were right," went on Johnny. "She is a spoiled child. But in a way it's not her fault, it's the fault of her dad and mum for letting her have everything she wants. She was quite nice, wasn't she, when we were eating the cake, don't you think?"

Lollipop grunted.

"But then the moment she couldn't get her own way, she flew off the handle, didn't she?"

Lollipop grunted again.

"I've been quite successful at training you," Johnny Skinner said to the pig.

"I wonder if I could train her?"

He might have felt doubtful if he could have witnessed the scene in the Palace that evening.

"Bedtime, Penelope," said the Queen.

"No," said the Princess.

"Tell her, Theo," said the Queen.

"Come on now, Penelope old girl," said the King. "You've had a long day, you must be tired."

"Am *not*. I don't want to go to bed yet. It's my birthday."

"Yes," said the Queen, "and you've had lots of presents, including a very special one from Daddy. Not many little girls get given a pig for a birthday present, and by the way, I haven't heard you thanking him yet. How about saying 'Thank you, Daddy' now?"

"Shan't. Not unless you let me stay up late."

"She could, couldn't she, Eth?" said the King. "Just this once? Just for a treat?"

"Oh I wash my hands of it!" cried the Queen, and she went to arrange some Royal roses in a Royal rose bowl.

"Till midnight, Daddy?" said the Princess.

"Well, all right then," said the King. "Just this once."

The Princess smiled a self-satisfied smile.

"Thanks," she said. "For the pig, I mean."

"I'm glad you like it, darling," said the King. "I'm sure it's very comfortable in its loose box."

"Oh you needn't think it's going to stay there for ever."

"What do you mean?" said the Queen, looking up from her roses.

"My pig," said Princess Penelope, "is going to be a house-pig. Or I suppose I should say, a palace-pig."

And then all the members of the Royal

household, from the Lord High Chamberlain to the smallest scullery boy, heard Queen Ethelwynne go off into screaming hysterics.

## CHAPTER FOUR

# "Busy! Understand?"

One thing you could say for certain about that spoiled child Princess Penelope – she didn't mess about.

Hardly had the grooms and stable-lads begun work in the Royal Mews next morning than the Princess appeared, making for the loose box in which her pig was kept.

Johnny Skinner had just returned from the Royal kitchens with a bucketful of tasty pigswill, and Lollipop was tucking in, snout deep in the trough.

"Johnny," said the Princess. "You think yourself a brilliant pig trainer, don't you? You could train Lollipop to do anything, I suppose?"

"Well, I don't know about that, miss," said Johnny. "I could train her to do most things, I suppose."

"But could you train her *not* to do *some* things?"

"How d'you mean, miss?"

"Could you train her not to do things in the house? Could you house-train her?"

"Well, she's never lived in a house."

"But she's going to live in one now," said

the Princess. "In fact she's going to live in the Palace, my pig is. So could you palace-train her?"

For a moment Johnny did not answer. He stood scratching his head and wondering if it would be possible.

Princess Penelope stamped her foot.

"Well?" she said. "Could you or couldn't you?"

With a pig as intelligent as Lollipop, Johnny thought, I reckon I could.

"I reckon I could, miss," he said, "but she'll have to stop in this loose box for a while yet, and then if she makes any mistakes, it won't matter. It'll take a bit of time."

"Well, don't waste any then," said the Princess sharply. "Get on with it." And off she went.

Thoughtfully, Johnny Skinner scratched Lollipop's bristly back, a back that seemed already to be getting plumper than it had been.

"What d'you think, old girl?" he said to her as she licked the last of her breakfast from the trough. "Do you think you could learn to be palace-trained?"

Lollipop grunted. To Johnny's ears, Lollipop had a whole vocabulary of different grunts that all, he was sure, meant different things: like "Scratch my back" or "Rub my ears" or (mostly) "I'm hungry".

But there were two distinct grunts that Johnny knew meant "Yes" or "No".

"Yes" was a quick, slightly high-pitched grunt. "No" was a deeper grunt, more long-drawn-out.

Now, in answer to Johnny's question, Lollipop clearly gave the "Yes" grunt.

"Right," said Johnny. "Then we'll give it a go. But if you're going to finish up palace-trained, you'll have to begin by becoming loose-box-trained," and he tied the old bit of rope round the pig's neck and opened the door into the yard outside.

First, thought Johnny, I must teach her a new word of command that she will learn to understand, just as she does with "Sit" or "Down".

He looked at Lollipop and saw that she was gazing up at him with bright, intelligent eyes, just as though she was aware of the thoughts that were going through his head, and suddenly he knew the word he was going to use.

He took the rope off her neck, pointed to a patch of grass on the far side of the yard and said to the pig, "Busy!"

Lollipop looked up at him again, then looked across the yard.

"Busy!" said Johnny again. "Understand?"

And Lollipop gave the quick, high-pitched

grunt, trotted over to the patch of grass, and did everything that Johnny wanted her to do.

## CHAPTER FIVE

# *"I'll jolly well make you a duke"*

Poor King Theophilus! He found himself between a rock and a hard place.

On one side was his daughter, quite determined that her new pet should be a palace-pig.

On the other, his wife, who, after her bout of hysterics upon learning of this, had served upon him the following ultimatum.

"If that ugly, dirty, stupid animal sets trotter inside these walls, Theo," the Queen had said, "then out I go. There isn't room for both of us."

"But my dear Eth," said the King, "we have two hundred and forty rooms in this Palace."

"Which," replied the Queen, "is not going to be turned into a pigsty."

Next morning, meeting his daughter as she returned from the Royal Mews, the King said to her, "You were joking, weren't you, Penelope? About your new pet, I mean. I forget its name."

"Lollipop."

"About Lollipop, becoming a palace-pig? It was just a joke, wasn't it?"

"No," said the Princess.

"But," said the King, "your mother does not wish it."

"Well I do, Daddy."

"But … but … but," said the King, "it'll make messes everywhere."

"No, it won't," said the Princess. "I am having it palace-trained."

"By that boy, d'you mean? I forget his name."

"Johnny Skinner. I have just given him orders about it. Lollipop should soon be able to leave the loose box and live with us."

"But Penelope," said the King, "if she does, your mother has said she will leave us."

"You must tell her not to, then," said the Princess Penelope. "After all, Daddy, your word is law."

She smiled sweetly.

"I always do everything you tell me, don't I?" she said.

King Theophilus took a deep breath.

"Well darling," he said, "I am telling you now – you cannot bring that pig into the Palace."

He waited nervously for the outburst that must surely follow. Would she go into a terrible sulk? Would she shout and yell at him? Would she throw things? Once, in a fury, she had kicked his shins. He drew back a pace or two.

But to his surprise the Princess only gave him another sweet smile.

"Didn't you hear what I said?" asked the King.

"Yes," said the Princess, "but I'm not going to take a blind bit of notice of it," and off she went.

The King shut himself in his study.

"What am I to do?" he said out loud. "Why must the child be so unreasonable? Who is there who might make her see sense? Wait though! What about that boy? Suppose I told him I didn't want the pig to be palace-trained? He'd be bound to do what I told him, wouldn't he?"

So he sent for Johnny Skinner.

Johnny, of course, had never been inside the Palace before, and now, as he followed the footman who had brought the message to the Mews, he looked around him in wonder at all the rich furnishings, at the ornaments of gold and silver, at the portraits of the King's ancestors looking down at him from the tapestried walls, and felt beneath his feet the thick softness of the priceless carpets upon which, if all went well, Lollipop would before long be walking.

"Come in! Come in!" cried the King in a hearty voice when the footman opened the door. "Sit down, Johnny my boy, make yourself comfortable. How are you? Well, I hope?"

"Yes, sir," said Johnny.

"And your pig?"

"She's well, sir," said Johnny, "but she's not my pig any more."

"No, of course not, quite so," said the King. "But though you're no longer her owner, you are nevertheless her trainer, are you not?"

"Yes."

"You teach her things, don't you?"

"Yes, sir," replied Johnny. "I'm teaching her something new now."

"What?"

"I'm house-training her."

"Palace-training, you mean?" said the King.

"Yes."

"Are you telling me that you'll be able to teach her never to … er … um … never to do anything indoors?"

"Yes, sir."

"Like a well-trained dog, you mean?"

Johnny nodded.

If he really can do that, thought the King, then Eth won't have anything to complain about. Maybe Penelope will get her own way, after all. Like she always does.

"Johnny," said the King. "Tell me honestly. Would you say that my daughter is a bit spoiled?"

"No."

"Oh. What would you say then?"

"That she is very spoiled indeed. She needs to be taught to think more about other people and less about herself."

Dead right, thought the King.

"Could you teach her, d'you think?" he said.

"I might be able to."

"If you can, Johnny," said King Theophilus, "I'll jolly well make you a duke."

∞———— CHAPTER SIX ————∞

## *"You always want to get your own way"*

A duke, thought Johnny as he left the Palace.
Duke of what? Duke Skinner sounds a bit
funny. Still, it would have to be a good thing.
I mean, dukes don't live in loose boxes, do
they? So I'd better work hard on this training

business – not only training the pig (which I think will be fairly easy) but also training the Princess (which I'm sure will be pretty difficult).

Back in the loose box, he sat down beside Lollipop and said to her, "What do you think? Could I train that girl to be less selfish and spoiled?"

The pig gave her "Yes" grunt.

"But how shall I start?" said Johnny.

At that very moment, in came Princess Penelope.

Johnny stood up and said to the pig "Stand", and the pig stood up.

The Princess looked round the floor of the loose box.

"The straw seems to be very clean," she said. "Have you just mucked out?"

"No, miss," said Johnny. "No need for that, you just watch." And he opened the door and called Lollipop out and said "Busy!"

The Princess watched, amazed, as the pig trotted across the yard to the patch of grass and performed perfectly.

"That's brilliant, Johnny!" the Princess said, and when the pig came back, she too said to her "Busy!"

The pig gave a deep, long-drawn-out grunt.

"No good saying that now, miss," said Johnny. "She's only just done it."

"Well then, sit!" said the Princess to the pig. Lollipop remained standing.

"*Why* won't she do what I tell her?" said Princess Penelope angrily. "Stupid animal!"

The Princess didn't notice, but Lollipop was watching her carefully. The pig put her head on one side as though she was listening to these words, and she fluttered her long white eyelashes. Johnny felt that if she'd had eyebrows, she would have raised them in surprise.

At that moment, he had an idea. "Look, miss," he said, "Lollipop isn't stupid. She just hasn't been trained to obey you, only me. But I might be able to train her to obey you too, if you would do something for me in return."

"Like what?"

"Well, to begin with, you could speak more politely to Lollipop," said Johnny (and to me, he thought). "Animals are very sensitive to the tone of people's voices. Try talking to her more gently, if you want her to obey you."

He knelt down in the straw on the far side of Lollipop and began to rub the roots of her ears.

"Now try telling her to sit again, miss," he said, and he ducked his head down behind the pig's.

Then, the moment that the Princess said "Sit" (in a more kindly voice), Johnny whispered the word into one of the pig's ears, and down she sat.

"She did it!" cried Princess Penelope. "I told her to do it and she did it! What shall I tell her to do next, Johnny?"

Johnny Skinner stood up, brushing bits of straw off his knees.

"That's enough to begin with, miss," he said.

"Is *not*!" cried the Princess, stamping her foot. "I want to make her do other things. Stand, Lollipop. *Stand! Will* you do what I say!" But the pig remained sitting, at the same time giving the "No" grunt in answer.

"Stand," said Johnny quietly, and she stood up.

Just as quietly, he said to the Princess, "You've got to learn to be more patient, you know, if you want your pig to obey you. No good shouting at her and losing your temper. Trouble with you is, you always want to get your own way."

This is the moment, he said to himself.

If she acts now like the spoiled little madam she is, then I'm never going to be able to do anything with her and she'll never mend her manners. And I'll never be a duke, what's more!

Johnny stood, the pig at his side, waiting for the outburst.

Opposite him, the Princess stood with a face like thunder.

Then, in the silence, Lollipop moved forward and came to stand before the Princess, gazing up into her face with bright eyes. The Princess, staring into those eyes, fringed with long white lashes and shining with intelligence, saw someone not so very different from herself looking back at her.

At that moment, though she herself did not realize it, Princess Penelope grew up a little bit.

She looked at Johnny Skinner, and Johnny smiled at her.

"All right, Johnny," she said. "I'll try to be more patient. With both of you."

"Good," said Johnny. "That's good, miss. Isn't it, Lollipop?" And the pig gave that quick, high-pitched grunt.

## CHAPTER SEVEN
## *"What a good girl!"*

"The next thing to do," said Johnny to
Lollipop once the Princess had gone, "is for
me to teach you to obey her. I shan't be
able to get away with whispering in your
ear every time. I've never used food rewards

with you before but I think this is the time to start," and he begged a small sack of pony-nuts from one of the stable-lads in the Mews.

When the Princess next visited the loose box, Johnny explained his plan to her.

"First, tell Lollipop to sit," he said, "which you're going to do in a nice voice, aren't you?"

The Princess nodded.

"And then," said Johnny, "if she doesn't obey you, simply turn your back on her. But if she does obey you, then give her a few pony-nuts and a lot of praise. Understand, miss?"

The Princess nodded.

So Johnny passed her a handful of the nuts, which she pocketed.

Then he in turn nodded directly at her.

Before them Lollipop stood, her eyes fixed on the girl. She had seen the handful of nuts –

she could smell them, she wanted them.

"Sit, Lollipop," said Princess Penelope in a quiet voice.

The pig remained standing.

The Princess turned her back on her pet.

Lollipop looked up at Johnny.

It was an enquiring look, a what-have-I-done-wrong look.

Johnny said nothing, but merely frowned and shook his head at the pig.

"Turn round now, miss," he said, "and try again."

The Princess turned.

"Sit," she said quietly once more.

Lollipop shot a glance at Johnny and saw that he was both smiling and nodding. She saw also that the Princess's hand had gone to her pocket.

The pig sat down.

"*What* a good pig!" cried the Princess, and

she held out some pony-nuts on the palm of her hand.

Lollipop took the nuts quite delicately, at the same time giving out a string of contented little grunts. Johnny, who understood her language pretty well, was fairly certain that she was saying, "Hey! This girl's not so bad after all. The boy has never rewarded me with food, but the girl is going to if I do what she tells me."

And so when the Princess said "Stand", the pig stood up and got some more nuts and a lot more praise.

"What command shall I try next, Johnny?" said the Princess, again in a quiet voice.

"I think we'd better just stick to S–I–T and S–T–A–N–D for the moment, miss," replied Johnny. "I'm spelling them," he said, "so as not to muddle her. Try another S–I–T."

So the Princess did, and the pig obeyed

immediately. Reward and praise followed, as they did after Lollipop just as promptly stood again when told.

After half a dozen sits and stands, Johnny said, "I think that's enough for today. We don't want her to get bored. She's done very well."

"What about *me*, Johnny?" said the Princess with just a touch of her old petulance.

"You've done well too, miss. Very well."

"Anyone would think you were training me!" laughed the Princess. "I'm surprised you didn't say '*What* a good girl!' and offer me some pony-nuts. When can I have my next lesson, Mr Skinner, sir?"

"Tomorrow, miss," Johnny said.

"I wish you'd stop calling me 'miss'," said the Princess.

"But you said you didn't mind."

"I don't, but why can't you call me by my name?"

"Call you Penelope, d'you mean?"

"Yes," said the Princess. "Think about it.
See you tomorrow."

Johnny thought about it. If I do call her
Penelope, he said to himself, she'll maybe get
angry and bite my head off. Likewise if I don't.
Can't win.

But then something told him that he would
be silly not to do as the Princess asked. It was
beginning to look as though she wasn't such
a bad sort of girl after all.

## CHAPTER EIGHT

## *"If the pig comes in, Mummy goes out"*

"Daddy," said the Princess that evening.

"Yes, my love?" replied King Theophilus.

"It won't be long now before Lollipop can come and live in the Palace."

The King looked nervously around in case

Queen Ethelwynne should have heard these words, but she was not in the room.

"Oh, Penelope, darling," said the King, "you can't do this. I told you, didn't I? If the pig comes in, Mummy goes out."

He waited, even more nervously, for the explosion that always followed if his daughter's wishes were thwarted.

To his surprise, the Princess replied, "Look Daddy, I promise you that my Lollipop will be perfectly palace-trained. Mummy has no need to worry."

What's come over her, thought the King, speaking in such a reasonable way?

"Johnny Skinner is training her to be a perfect palace-pig," said the Princess, "and what's more, he's training me too."

"Training you?"

"Yes, to be a bit more patient and not to shout and lose my temper. He said I always want to get my own way."

"Did he indeed?" said the King.

He remembered what Johnny had said to him – "She needs to be taught to think more about other people and less about herself."

"Penelope darling," he said. "I do hope that you will change your mind about bringing your pig into the Palace, however well-trained it becomes."

The Princess smiled.

"No, Daddy dear, I shan't change my mind," she said. "You'll just have to change Mummy's."

That evening, the King tried.

"Eth dear," he said. "About Penelope's pig..."

"What about Penelope's pig?" said the Queen in a dangerously quiet voice. "Don't imagine for one moment, Theophilus, that you can persuade me to change my mind and allow that ugly, dirty, stupid animal into my Palace."

"But…" said the King.

"No buts," said the Queen. "I'm going to bed. Good night."

To begin with, it was not a good night for the King as he tossed and turned beneath the tufted tester of the great Royal four-poster bed, unable to sleep. His thoughts ran round and round the same track. Penelope was going to bring the pig into the Palace. Then Eth would leave it. What a scandal there would be throughout the kingdom! Everyone, from the Lord High Chamberlain to the smallest scullery boy, would know that Queen Ethelwynne had upped and left King Theophilus. And why? Because the King had allowed the Princess Penelope to bring her pet pig to live in the Palace.

Half the populace would say, "And I don't

blame the Queen!" and the other half would blame him, saying, "What sort of a king is he if he can't control his own little daughter?"

The fact is, nobody can control her, thought the King wearily, lying and listening to the Queen's soft snores. But then, towards dawn, it suddenly occurred to him that there was somebody who could control her! Johnny Skinner!

Very carefully, so as not to wake the Queen, King Theophilus got out of bed.

Like all people who work with animals, the grooms and stable-lads in the Royal Mews began their duties very early in the day. It was barely light when, to their great surprise, they saw entering the mews the figure of the King, in dressing-gown, nightshirt and carpet slippers, on the Royal head not a crown but a tasselled nightcap.

All took care to pretend to be unaware of

his presence, but out of the corners of their eyes they saw him enter the loose box in which the Princess's pig was kept.

Inside, the pig lay in the straw alone, for Johnny had already left to collect all last night's scraps from the Royal kitchens.

As the King came in, the pig stood up. A gesture of respect, the King thought, though in fact Lollipop had supposed it was Johnny, coming with her breakfast.

I must say, thought the King, she looks twice the pig she was.

"Good morning, Lollipop," he said. "I trust you are well?" He was answered by a quick, high-pitched grunt from the pig, who stood before him, gazing up into his face with bright eyes.

The King, staring into those eyes, fringed with long white lashes and shining with intelligence, saw someone not so very different from himself looking back. The pig, it seemed to the King, even fluttered her eyelashes at him.

Just then Johnny came in with the swill bucket, and Lollipop let out a loud squeal, the meaning of which was plain even to the King.

"Excuse me, sir," said Johnny. "Can't keep her ladyship waiting," and he sloshed the food into the trough.

Her ladyship, thought the King as he watched the pig tucking in. If the boy can find a way out of the mess I'm in, I'll not only make him a duke, I'll award her the title of Lady Lollipop.

"How's the training going, Johnny?" he asked.

"I'll show you, sir," said Johnny, "just as soon as she's finished," and when she had, he opened the door, called her out and told her to be busy.

"See, sir?" said Johnny as they watched. "No problem. She could move into the Palace tomorrow."

## *"Wipe your feet"*

"Amazing!" said the King. "But still, she'd bring a lot of muck in on her feet, wouldn't she? Mud all over the carpets, I mean?"

"I'd thought of that, sir," said Johnny, and he produced a large doormat which he laid down in front of the pig.

"Wipe your feet," he told her, and at these words Lollipop walked forward and scraped first her front trotters and then the back ones on the mat.

"Astonishing!" said the King. "But then how's she going to get out when she wants to? There may not always be someone to open the door for her, like you just did."

"I'd thought of that too," said Johnny, and he unrolled a scroll of paper upon which he had drawn a diagram. It was a picture of a door, an ordinary door, except that in the middle of the lower half of it there was a pig-sized section that had been cut out and hinged at its top, to swing either way.

"It's a pig-flap, d'you see?" said Johnny. "When Lollipop wants to go out, she'll push with her snout at the bottom of the flap and it'll swing open and through she'll go, and she'll come back in the same way. She'll be independent."

"Astounding!" said the King.

"You have a door leading to the Royal Gardens, sir, I suppose?" asked Johnny.

"Oh, yes."

"The Palace carpenters could soon put a pig-flap in that, working from my design. Then you'd have nothing to worry about, sir. Lollipop goes into the garden when she needs to and wipes her feet when she comes back in."

"Oh but Johnny," said the King, "the Royal Gardens are the Queen's pride and joy. She doesn't much like digging, you know, too much like hard work, but she especially loves her rose-garden. Roses are her favourite flowers and she's never happier than when she's picking them or pruning them or dead-heading them. Just think of the damage that pig could do in the Royal Gardens!"

"An ordinary pig, yes, sir," said Johnny. "I quite agree. But just think of the good that a very intelligent, highly trained pig like Lollipop could do. At one end she could turn over the soil in the flower borders and plough up the vegetable patch with her snout, and at the other end – well, pig dung is very good for roses, sir. It would be easy for me to teach Lollipop to be busy in the rose-garden. You never know, she might become quite popular with the Queen, and then—"

"And then," interrupted the King, "she might be allowed into the Palace! Johnny, you're a genius!"

He looked at Lollipop, who was still snuffling round her trough in case she'd missed anything, and then he said, "Gosh! I'm hungry! Have you had your breakfast, Johnny?"

"No, sir," replied Johnny.

"Well, come back home with me and we'll all have breakfast together."

By now it was broad daylight, of course, and there were plenty of people about to see the King, in dressing-gown and nightshirt and carpet slippers, on his head not a crown but a tasselled nightcap, walking back to the Palace in earnest conversation with the boy who looked after Princess Penelope's pig.

"I feel like having my favourite breakfast," the King was saying to Johnny. "Scrambled eggs on fried bread. Does that sound all right to you?"

"It certainly does," said Johnny.

Back in the Palace, they found the Queen and the Princess at the breakfast table.

"You remember Johnny, Eth?" said the King.

"I do," said the Queen. "Though it is something of a surprise to see him here."

You wait, thought the King, you may be

getting a bigger surprise before long, and he gave orders for the two breakfasts – "As quick as you can, we're starving."

"Are you not going to dress, Theo?" asked the Queen.

"Later, my dear, later. Now then Johnny, sit down. Sit beside Penelope there."

Johnny sat down, opposite the Queen, who, he could see, was looking very disapprovingly at him over a great bowl of roses that stood in the middle of the table. He leaned across to sniff at them.

"My favourite flowers," he said.

The Queen's expression softened a little.

"But," said Johnny, "never in my life have I seen such beautiful ones. Please ma'am," he said to the Queen, "what variety are they?"

The beginnings of a smile appeared on the Queen's face. "They are a new hybrid," she said, "grown especially for me. In fact they are called Ethelwynne's Beautiful."

"How true, ma'am," said Johnny, and the
Queen inclined her head, smiling broadly now.

"So you like roses, do you?" she said.

"Oh yes, ma'am," said Johnny. "I would
love to see your rose-garden."

"Get this lot down you first, Johnny," said
the King as two huge platefuls appeared, "and
then I'm sure the Queen will show you round
afterwards, won't you, Eth?"

The Queen, her own breakfast finished,
stood up.

"Come and find me when you're ready,
boy," she said, and she left the room.

"Just what's going on, Daddy?" asked
the Princess. "What have you been up to,
wandering around in your nightclothes? Have
you and Johnny been hatching some plan?"

"We have," they both replied, and they
told her about the doormat and the pig-flap,

and the scheme for making Lollipop useful in the Royal Gardens, so that hopefully the Queen would come round to the idea of her becoming a palace-pig.

"Things are looking good, Penelope," the King said. "It looks as though Mummy's already taken quite a shine to Johnny. The next step is to make her like his pig."

"*My* pig, Daddy!" said the Princess sharply.

"Sorry, sorry, your pig, darling," said the King hastily. He too now got up from the table, rubbing his tummy appreciatively, and went out of the room.

Johnny swallowed his last mouthful.

"That was lovely, miss," he said.

"*Not* 'miss', Johnny, remember?"

Perhaps because he was so pleasantly full of scrambled eggs and fried bread Johnny replied, easily and naturally, "Oh sorry, Penelope."

The Princess smiled.

"Come on, I'll show you the way to Mummy's rose-garden," she said.

She's got a nice smile, Johnny Skinner thought as he followed.

# *"She had better come in to tea"*

That night, as the King and the Queen lay
side by side beneath the tufted tester of the
great Royal four-poster bed, the Queen said,
"You know, Theo, that boy Johnny knows a
lot about roses."

"Does he indeed, Eth?" said the King.

"Yes, he knows all the different types, the hybrid teas, the floribundas, the climbers, the ramblers, and which months they flower in and which ones are resistant to disease. He's not just a swineherd, he's a bright boy."

"Good, good," said the King. "Did he talk to you at all about Lollipop?"

"I presume you mean that pig."

"Yes."

"Certainly not. The boy has sense enough to know that I do not approve of the creature."

There was a longish silence, during which the King considered the idea of having a proper row with the Queen about Penelope's pig. After all, I am the King, he thought. Everyone has to do what I tell them. Even the Queen. But, he said to himself, if we do have a row about it, I know who'll win, and it won't be me.

Just then the Queen said sleepily, "I might find a job for that boy in the garden."

"Good, good," said the King.

The Queen yawned.

"Good night, Theo," she said.

"Good night, Eth."

After a few minutes the Queen said, "I've been meaning to ask you – why ever did you come down to breakfast in your nightclothes?"

"Must have overslept," said the King.

"Funny," the Queen said drowsily. "There were bits of straw in your carpet slippers."

The King said nothing, hoping that she would not next say "Why was that?", but then he heard a small snore and he settled down thankfully. Soon his deeper snores accompanied hers.

In her mini-four-poster the Princess

Penelope dreamed pleasant dreams. Johnny came into them, but they were mostly about her pig. In them Lollipop did all sorts of fantastic things that she, Penelope, had taught her to do, like playing the piano and walking on her hind legs and sitting up at the table with a napkin round her neck.

In the loose box, on a mattress made of sacks stuffed with straw, Johnny Skinner's dreams were also pleasant ones. Penelope appeared in them, but they were mostly about Lollipop. In one of them she was carefully using her snout to turn over the earth between the rose-bushes while the Queen watched approvingly, saying, "*What a good pig!*"

Beside Johnny, deep in the straw, Lollipop, full-stomached, slept dreamlessly.

Next morning Johnny was summoned to the Palace again. The King was in his study and the Princess was also there. They looked rather pleased with themselves, Johnny thought, as though they were sharing a secret.

"Sit down, Johnny my boy," said the King, and then, "Go on, Penelope, tell him."

"Johnny," said the Princess, "we want you to bring Lollipop to the Royal Gardens after lunch today."

"Does your mother know?" asked Johnny.

"No, and she won't be back till teatime because she's going out this afternoon."

"To a flower show," said the King. "She has entered a bunch of Ethelwynne's Beautiful in the Hybrid Tea Class."

"And if she wins," said the Princess, "she'll be in such a good mood that perhaps she won't mind about my pig being in the garden, especially if Lollipop has done useful things among the roses. If she doesn't mind her in the garden, maybe she won't mind her in the Palace."

"Bring the pig in through the gates at the bottom of the Royal Gardens, Johnny," said the King, "and then if things don't go right, you can slip out again the same way."

Johnny thought for a minute.

"But suppose things do go right, sir," he said, "might it be a good idea to have the pig-flap ready? The Royal carpenters could make a new door with the flap in it, but leave the old door where it is. Then, if things go according to plan, they could quickly hang the new door and we could demonstrate the whole thing, doormat and all, to the Queen. What d'you think, sir?"

"I think," said the King, "that you may be one step nearer to your dukedom."

So it was that that afternoon the King and

the Princess and Johnny and Lollipop all met beside the Queen's rose-garden. Beside the old door that led out from the Palace into the Royal Gardens a footman stood waiting, with orders to report the Queen's return. Concealed behind some curtains, the Royal carpenters waited, ready to substitute the new door with the pig-flap in it, should a signal come later from the rose-garden.

Now came the moment to show what Johnny had been training the pig to do in an old patch of rough ground within the Royal Mews. He led her into the rose-garden and gave the command "Rootle". At this the pig put her head down and with her snout began to grub up the soil between the rose-bushes, turning it all over, burying the weeds, and sifting through the earth to make a fine tilth.

She worked her way methodically round and round the circular rose-garden, being careful not to disturb the bushes, until the whole large expanse had been thoroughly cultivated, far more thoroughly than any human gardener could have done.

When Lollipop had finished, she stood looking up at the three watchers, who with one voice cried, "*What* a good pig!"

Then, as Johnny was wiping the earth from her snout, the footman came running from the garden door.

"Your Majesty!" he panted. "Her Majesty has returned, may it please Your Majesty."

"Right," said the King. "Now you keep your eye on me, my good man, and if – and only if – I hold both arms up as if I were stretching, you understand, you tell those carpenters to swap the doors."

"Quick, Johnny," said the Princess. "Get Lollipop out of sight. Hide behind that privet hedge. Don't come out unless I call you."

Then she and her father waited anxiously for the Queen to emerge.

When she did, they saw at once that she wore, pinned upon her dress, one small and one large red rosette.

"Guess what!" she cried happily as she hurried towards them. "I won!"

"What did you win, Eth?" asked the King.

"First Prize in the Hybrid Tea Class!" said the Queen.

"But you've got two rosettes, Mummy," said the Princess.

"Yes!" cried the Queen. "Because my Ethelwynne's Beautifuls won Best in Show!" and she broke into a little dance of joy.

Then she saw her rose-bed.

"Oh!" she cried. "How very professionally my rose-garden has been dug and weeded!"

"Hasn't it just!" said the King, and "Johnny!" called the Princess, and Johnny Skinner appeared from behind the privet hedge, followed by Lollipop.

"Whatever is that pig doing here?" said the Queen.

"She's been cultivating your rose-garden, ma'am," said Johnny. "Haven't you, Lollipop?" and the pig gave her "Yes" grunt.

"She did it all, Mummy," said the Princess. "She did it all, by herself."

Then she said "Come, Lollipop" and the pig came to her, and "Sit", and the pig sat, gazing up into the Queen's face with bright eyes.

The Queen, staring into those eyes, fringed with long white lashes and shining with intelligence, saw someone not so very different from herself looking back at her.

"Did you really?" said the Queen to Lollipop. "Do it all? By yourself?"

In reply there came a quick, high-pitched grunt.

"*What* a good pig," said Queen Ethelwynne softly. "She must be tired after all that work, and thirsty too. She had better come in to tea." And the King held both his arms up as if he were stretching.

## CHAPTER ELEVEN

# I'll give the boy a job

"Come along in then, all of you," said the Queen.

But Johnny could see that they needed to play for time – the carpenters had not yet completed the exchange of doors.

"Excuse me, ma'am," he said to the Queen. "Lollipop may need to make herself comfortable before we go indoors."

"Oh let me tell her, Johnny!" cried the Princess. "I haven't got any pony-nuts on me, but she did sit when I told her to just now. Let me try, can I?"

Johnny nodded, and with that Penelope said to Lollipop (in a bright, encouraging voice), "Busy! Good pig, busy!"

As the Queen watched in amazement, the pig marched back into the centre of the rose-garden and deposited a generous supply of pig dung at the foot of a fine floribunda.

"Just the stuff for growing prize roses, ma'am," said Johnny quietly to the Queen.

"She did it!" cried the Princess. "She did it when I told her to, Johnny! Did you see, Mummy? Did you see, Daddy? It isn't only Johnny she obeys, it's me too!" And confidently she called "Come, Lollipop" and Lollipop came, and then "Heel!" and Lollipop walked sedately to heel beside the Princess, followed by the King and Johnny and a mystified Queen.

Even more mystified was she when they reached the Palace's garden door, for she could see how different it now looked.

"What is that, in the door?" she asked.

"It's a pig-flap, Mummy," said the Princess. "It's an invention of Johnny's. Lollipop will be able to go in and out as she likes."

"But her feet…" said the Queen, looking at the pig's muddy trotters.

"Don't worry, ma'am," said Johnny. "If you will all go inside, you'll see."

So the Royal Family all went in through the new garden door while Johnny kept Lollipop sitting beside him outside.

Once they had closed the door behind

them, Johnny called "Right" and, from inside, the Princess called "Come, Lollipop" and the pig pushed open the pig-flap with her snout and entered.

"Wipe your feet," commanded the Princess, and then carefully her pig wiped her trotters, one after another, on the doormat.

How they praised the Princess's pig, and how they laughed when the pig-flap swung open again and through it, on hands and knees and grunting loudly, came Johnny Skinner, grinning all over his face.

After that, everything went swimmingly. As they made their way through the Palace, Lollipop, walking close at heel beside the Princess, made a series of strange little noises, snuffles, chuckles and chortles, as she looked around her in wonder at all the rich furnishings, at the ornaments of gold and silver, at the portraits of the King's ancestors looking down at her from the tapestried walls, and felt beneath her trotters the thick softness of the priceless carpets upon which, though she did not know it, she would in future always be able to walk.

And at teatime the pig behaved perfectly. She didn't exactly sit up at the table with a napkin round her neck as Penelope had dreamed, but she ate toasted buttered teacake from a silver dish as delicately as a lady.

"So what d'you think, Eth?" asked the King.

"What do I think about what?" asked the Queen.

"About Lollipop."

"I hardly know what I think," replied the Queen, fingering the two red rosettes she wore. "Today has been so extraordinary. But Penelope's pig is certainly a most remarkable animal."

"With a most remarkable trainer by the name of Johnny Skinner," said the King.

"And a most remarkable owner," cried the Princess, "who is now going to keep her pet pig in the Palace, but only, of course, if her mother says that she can.

"Please, Mummy?"

Johnny and the King both looked at the Princess and each thought, What a cunning girl!

The Queen looked at her daughter and thought how she had changed. Gone were the sulks and the shouting and the selfishness, and instead here was this happy, jolly little girl. How had it happened? It must be something to do with that boy.

"Can I, Mummy?" the Princess said again. "Can I keep her here?"

The Queen fed another teacake to the pig.

"We'll see," she said.

King and Princess looked at one another

and father winked at daughter. The battle was won, they knew, but each was thinking, What about Johnny?

"What about Johnny, Eth?" said King Theophilus.

"What about him?"

"Well, he can't spend the rest of his life in a loose box, not after all he's done for us, in the way of helping Penelope – with her pig, I mean."

It *is* something to do with that boy, thought Queen Ethelwynne, and just as though she could read that thought, Lollipop turned to the Queen and made her high-pitched "Yes" grunt.

I thought as much, said the Queen to herself. It's he who has made Penelope so much more reasonable. And my roses – he's so good on roses. And that pig – cultivator and dung-spreader rolled into one. I'll give the boy a job.

"Well?" said the King.

"Well?" said the Princess.

"Well," said the Queen, "I could do with some help in the garden. And there's a cottage vacant. It's very small, but cosy. How would you like to be my under-gardener, Johnny?"

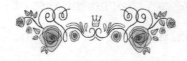

## CHAPTER TWELVE

## *"Lady Lollipop!"*

The news travelled fast in the Palace,
and soon everyone, from the Lord High
Chamberlain to the smallest scullery boy,
knew that Princess Penelope's pet was now a
palace-pig, sleeping on a sheepskin rug at the

foot of her mistress's mini-four-poster and, should the need arise, making her way down the Grand Staircase, out through the pig-flap, and on to the rose-bed.

They knew also that the Queen had a new under-gardener with whom she talked endlessly about flower-beds and borders, and lawns and lily-ponds, and, especially, about roses.

And all of them saw how much happier the Royal Family was, now that the Princess was no longer a spoiled child, but a happy pig-keeper.

One evening, a lovely summer's evening, the King and the Queen were sitting out in the gardens, watching their daughter training her pig, when they saw Johnny come out of his little cottage beyond the vegetable patch.

"Penelope!" they heard him call. "Where are you, Penelope?"

"Did you hear that, Theo?" said the Queen. "Isn't it a bit much that Johnny Skinner, a commoner, should address the Princess by name?"

"I shouldn't worry, Eth," the King said. "I'm going to make him a duke."

"Honestly, Theo," said the Queen, laughing. "Next thing, you'll be ennobling the pig!"

"I shall," said the King, as they sat and watched their daughter and her pig running to meet the boy who had been the owner of one and was the playmate of the other. "I *shall* be making her a lady. Lady Lollipop!"

# Contents

CHAPTER ONE ~ 102
"She ought to have a governess"

CHAPTER TWO ~ 113
"Your daughter is
very strong-minded"

CHAPTER THREE ~ 125
"He's a sort of magician"

CHAPTER FOUR ~ 135
"I'll jolly well make you a duke"

CHAPTER FIVE ~ 142
"Bird droppings and
slug slime and mashed
mouse manure"

CHAPTER SIX ~ 149
"How would you
like to be Penny?"

CHAPTER SEVEN ~ *155*
*"The facts I'm going
to learn today"*

CHAPTER EIGHT ~ *160*
*"A moly is a magic herb"*

CHAPTER NINE ~ *169*
*"Anything to stop you all nagging me"*

CHAPTER TEN ~ *176*
*"Good old Lady Lollipop"*

CHAPTER ELEVEN ~ *184*
*"Dark and handsome"*

CHAPTER TWELVE ~ *191*
*"Oh, Collie, you fixed it!"*

CHAPTER THIRTEEN ~ *203*
*"What a lovely surprise!"*

## CHAPTER ONE

## *"She ought to have a governess"*

Once upon a time, in a faraway land, a king sat thinking at the big table in the grand banqueting-hall of his great Palace. His name was King Theophilus, and he was thinking, with pleasure, of the breakfast that was shortly to be brought to him. It was his favourite breakfast – scrambled eggs on fried bread.

In the garden-room, so called because its French windows gave a perfect view of the Royal rose-garden, his wife, Queen Ethelwynne, sat thinking. She was thinking, with pleasure, of the lovely blooms which she could see outside, especially those of a particular rose called Ethelwynne's Beautiful.

Princess Penelope, daughter of the King and the Queen, sat in a room still called the nursery, though she was now too old to need a nursemaid, thinking, with pleasure, about her friend Johnny Skinner and her pig Lollipop. She spent a good deal of her time thinking about one or the other, perhaps because both of them – though maybe she did not realize this – had made a great deal of difference to her and changed her, greatly for the better.

Princess Penelope had been a selfish, rude and stubborn child, much spoiled by her father, and a real pain in the neck to all and sundry. She had demanded a pet as an eighth birthday present, and not just any old pet but a pig.

She had chosen one belonging to a very poor boy by the name of Johnny Skinner. "Lollipop" he called this pig, and he had taught her to do all manner of clever tricks. He had even taught her to be house-trained, or rather palace-trained, for the Princess was determined that Lollipop should be treated just like a pet dog or cat and should sleep at the foot of her bed.

King Theophilus, of course, gave in to everything his daughter wanted. Queen Ethelwynne was a harder nut to crack, but even she was won over when Johnny trained Lollipop to dig over the Royal rose-beds with her snout at his command of "Rootle!" and

when he said "Busy!" she would fertilize
the roses with her dung, which she would
deposit at the foot of each bush.

Equally importantly from the Queen's
point of view, the pig was perfectly palace-
trained, and Johnny Skinner was offered the
job of under-gardener and a little cottage to
go with it.

Now, as the King was thinking about
breakfast and the Queen about roses and the
Princess about him, Johnny sat in his little
cottage, thinking about his pig.

It's her pig now, he thought, I know that
in my mind, but in my heart Lollipop will
always be mine. Perhaps the best way to look
at it is that Penelope thinks she's hers and
I think she's mine, so she's ours.

Now Johnny was not a boastful sort of
boy, but he knew that it was due to him that
Princess Penelope had changed from a spoiled

child to a much nicer sort of girl, of whom he'd grown quite fond.

But she should be at school, he thought, learning things. I never went to school, so what little I know I've picked up as I've gone along. For example, I've never learned to read.

Thinking about reading somehow made him think about weeding (something I know how to do, he said to himself with a smile), and he went out into the garden and started work. I wonder, he thought, if Penelope can read properly. She ought to have a governess.

At that moment, Queen Ethelwynne came out through her French windows and walked along a path towards the bed in which Johnny was working. Good boy, she thought, he's doing just what I was going to ask him to do.

"Good morning, Johnny," she said.

Johnny scrambled to his feet.

"Good morning, Your Majesty," he replied.

"When you've finished that," said the Queen, "would you put Lollipop through the rose-beds? They could do with turning over."

"Yes, ma'am," said Johnny.

Lollipop's ideal for roses, he thought, she cultivates them with her front end and fertilizes them with her back end. Should I put it like that to Her Majesty? No, perhaps not.

"I've been reading a new book on roses, Johnny," said Queen Ethelwynne. "Would you like to borrow it when I've finished?"

"Kind of you, ma'am," said Johnny, "but I've never been taught to read."

"What!" said the Queen. "How awful for you! Reading is so important."

My chance, thought Johnny. She seems in a good mood. I'll try my luck.

"Princess Penelope is a great reader, I expect, ma'am?" he said.

Ho-hum, thought the Queen, he's very

sharp, this boy. I'll see what he has to say.

"In fact," she replied, "Her Royal Highness is not all that interested in books."

"Is that so?" said Johnny. "I've never been to school, of course."

"As a matter of fact," said the Queen, "nor has the Princess."

They looked at one another.

"Are you suggesting something, Johnny?" asked the Queen.

"Yes," said Johnny. "She ought to have a governess."

A few minutes later Queen Ethelwynne burst into the great banqueting-hall, where King Theophilus was still sitting at the big table, eating the last mouthful of a second helping of scrambled eggs on fried bread.

"Theo!" said the Queen.

"Yes, Eth?" said the King, swallowing hastily and mopping his mouth with his napkin.

"I've been thinking. About Penelope. And I've made up my mind."

"Yes, Eth?" said the King.

"She ought to have a governess."

Meanwhile, in the nursery, Lollipop had a problem. Palace-trained she might be, but the morning was drawing on and she had not yet been let out into the garden.

Princess Penelope should, of course, have done this ages ago, but she was in a sort of daydream, thinking about her two friends.

Maybe Johnny still reckons that Lollipop is his, she said to herself, but she's not, she's mine. Perhaps the best way to look at it is that she's ours.

Suddenly she became aware that the pig was standing close beside her, and then she heard a snuffle and felt a nudge against her leg.

"What's the matter, Lollipop?" asked the Princess, looking into the pig's bright intelligent eyes and seeing someone very like herself looking back.

For answer, Lollipop trotted across to the door of the nursery.

"Oh sorry!" cried the Princess. "You want to go out, is that it?" And in reply the pig gave the one short sharp grunt that meant, as both her owners knew, "Yes".

Quickly Princess Penelope opened the nursery door, and quickly both Princess and pig ran down the corridor that ended in a door which led to the garden.

"Busy!" said the Princess.

Johnny, looking up from his weeding, saw Lollipop rush to the rose-beds.

Once she's made herself comfortable, he thought, I might as well put her straight to work. So he waited until all had been done that needed to be done, and then he called out to the Princess.

"Penelope!" he cried. "Your mother wants Lollipop put through the rose-beds. Can you start her while I'm finishing this weeding?"

"Right-ho, Duke," called Princess Penelope.

Just as Johnny had given up addressing the Princess as "Your Royal Highness" (because she'd asked him to), so now she very often called her friend "Duke" (because King Theophilus had said he would make Johnny one, though actually he'd forgotten to do anything about it).

Now the Princess said to Lollipop "Rootle!" and the pig began to turn over the earth with her snout.

"Thanks, Penelope!" called Johnny. "I'll have finished this weeding in a minute."

Thinking about weeding somehow made him think about reading, and he said,

"Lollipop will work on her own. You can go and read a book if you like."

"I don't want to read some old book, Duke," the Princess replied.

You wait, Johnny Skinner said to himself. I've told your mother what I think you need and she'll have told your father and he'll do whatever your mother tells him, and before you can say "Jack Robinson" you'll be being taught to read. By your governess. I wonder what she'll be like?

## CHAPTER TWO

# *"Your daughter is very strong-minded"*

In the old days, that is to say before Johnny
Skinner and the pig called Lollipop came on
the scene, neither King nor Queen would
have stood the faintest chance of persuading
the Princess Penelope to have a governess.

"Will not!" she would have shouted, and that would have been that.

But now, the King and the Queen said to one another, their daughter was quite a different child. She would certainly see the benefit of having someone to teach her. They sent a footman to fetch her.

He found her in the garden, playing with her pig.

"Excuse me, Your Royal Highness," said the footman. "Their Majesties would like to have a word with you, they said. In the Royal drawing-room."

"All right," said the Princess. "Tell them I'll be there in half a tick."

She spent a little time scratching Lollipop's back and telling her how beautiful she was, and then she made her way in through the garden door (that had a special pig-flap fitted in it for Lollipop's use). The pig followed, carefully wiping her trotters on the mat inside as she had been trained to do. Then she walked at heel as Princess Penelope made her way to the drawing-room.

At sight of her the King, who had been sitting down, stood up, and the Queen, who had been standing up, sat down.

"Good morning, darling," they said with one voice.

"Morning Mummy, morning Daddy," the Princess said. "What d'you want?"

"Tell her, Theo," said the Queen.

"No, you tell her, Eth," said the King.

"Tell me what?" asked the Princess.

"Well," said the Queen, smiling sweetly at her daughter, "Daddy and I thought that, now you're such a big girl and so sensible and well behaved, it's time you had someone to help you."

"Help me?" said the Princess. "Help me to do what?"

"To learn things, darling," said the King, beaming broadly at his daughter. "Like reading and writing and arithmetic. We think you'd enjoy having someone to teach you."

"We think," said the Queen, "that you should have a governess. What do you say to that?"

There was a moment's silence, and King and Queen saw that their little daughter was frowning. Oh no, each thought, is it going to be like it used to be? They waited with bated breath for her to shout "Will not!" or to express point-blank refusal of this idea in one way or another.

What they did not expect was that the Princess should make no answer to her mother's question. Instead she turned to the pig, still standing at heel.

"A governess, Lollipop," said the Princess. "Would that be a good idea?"

Lollipop raised her head to look into the girl's eyes. Then she looked at the King. Then she looked at the Queen. Then she gave the short sharp "Yes" grunt.

The Princess turned back to face her anxious parents.

"I'll think about it," she said.

Then she left the drawing-room, the pig following, and made her way back to the garden where Johnny was hard at work.

"You'll never guess," she said to him. "They want me to have a governess."

"Really?" said Johnny.

"Yes," said the Princess. "Just imagine, having to do lessons."

"You're lucky," Johnny said.

"Lucky?"

"Yes. I never had any education but you'll be able to learn all sorts of things. Specially if they get you a really good governess.

You're fortunate, Penelope, you are."

"Hm," said the Princess. She thought for a moment. "Tell you what, Johnny," she said. "You could share her with me."

"I don't know," said Johnny, "that your mother and father would like that."

"They will," replied Princess Penelope, "because I'll tell them that I won't have any old governess unless you can have lessons too. That'll fix 'em, won't it, Lollipop?" And the pig grunted "Yes".

Of course the King and the Queen both said "Yes" to the idea of Johnny Skinner having lessons too. To say "No", each realized, would have been most unwise, and so King Theophilus issued a Royal Proclamation, inviting applicants for the post of Governess-to-the-Princess.

On the occasion of Princess Penelope's

eighth birthday, dozens of different pigs had been paraded in the Great Park for the Princess to choose one. During the next week dozens of women came to the Palace to be interviewed by the King and the Queen.

There were big ladies and middle-sized ladies and little ladies, some tall, some short, some fat, some thin, all very keen to be selected as Governess-to-the-Princess.

In the end the King and the Queen picked a retired schoolteacher by the name of Miss Gristle. (Or rather, the Queen picked her and the King agreed.)

Miss Gristle was tall and thin with iron-grey hair and a beaky nose, so that she looked like some sort of long-legged bird.

What had been the Princess's nursery was renamed the schoolroom, and in it, at Miss Gristle's request, were now three desks (a large one for her and two smaller ones for the children) and a blackboard.

There was a supply of chalk for the blackboard, and paper and pencils for the children, and on the walls were a map of the world and a large placard showing all the letters of the alphabet and another with all the numbers up to a hundred.

All was ready for the first morning's schooling.

It did not start too well.

Miss Gristle sat at her large desk awaiting the arrival of her Royal pupil, when the door of the schoolroom opened and in came the Princess and a long-legged boy.

"Good morning, Penelope," said Miss Gristle. And to Johnny she said, "Shut the door, please."

"Half a tick," said the Princess, "we're not all here yet." And then in through the schoolroom door came a short-legged pig.

At sight of Lollipop, Miss Gristle let out a piercing scream.

"It's a pig!" she cried.

"Full marks," said Penelope. "Well done, you."

"Take it away, take it away. I can't stand pigs!" cried the Governess-to-the-Princess.

"Suit yourself," said Penelope, "but if Lollipop goes, we go too. One out, all out!"

The one that went out, however, was Miss Gristle, her horrified eyes fixed upon the pig as though it had been a woman-eating tiger.

"Silly old thing," said Princess Penelope. "Isn't she, Duke?"

"I must say," replied Johnny Skinner, "I thought you were a bit hard on her. Now she'll probably give in her notice."

"Good," said the Princess.

"But Penelope," said Johnny, "it isn't

just you who needs a governess. I do too, remember?"

He turned to Lollipop.

"And you do, don't you, my lady?" And for answer the pig gave a volley of those short sharp "Yes" grunts.

Meanwhile Miss Gristle had sought out the King and Queen.

"Your Majesties!" she cried. "Penelope has brought a pig into my schoolroom!"

"Well, it's her pig," said the King.

"But," said the Queen, "it's not necessarily your schoolroom if you see fit to address our daughter by her Christian name in that familiar manner. You may call the boy 'Johnny' and the pig's name is 'Lady Lollipop', but perhaps you will remember in future to refer to our daughter as 'Princess Penelope' or, if you wish, as 'Her Royal Highness'."

Miss Gristle's mouth fell open, but no words came from it.

"And now," said the Queen, "perhaps you would return to your duties." And she swept out of the room.

"Sorry about all this," said the King as he prepared to follow her, "but don't worry about the pig. You'll soon get used to her."

"I shall not, sir," said Miss Gristle in a strangled voice. "I am leaving your employment. Now." And she too swept out.

King Theophilus made his way to the schoolroom, to find his daughter and Johnny Skinner sitting at their desks and Lady Lollipop sitting on the floor.

"Where's old Gristly gone, Daddy?" asked Penelope.

"She has given in her notice."

"Good," said the Princess. "I don't like her

and I don't think Johnny does and I'm certain Lady Lollipop doesn't – she kept giving that long deep grunt that means 'No'."

"Your daughter," said the King to his wife later, "is very strong-minded."

"And who does she get that from?" asked the Queen.

"Me?" said the King hopefully.

"If you believe that," said the Queen, "then you'd probably believe that Lollipop might come flying by the window any moment now. Find the child another governess, Theo, and be quick about it."

## CHAPTER THREE

*"He's a sort of magician"*

Find another governess, thought the King. It isn't finding one, it's keeping one that's going to be the problem. Suppose Penelope upsets the next one? What should I do? Who could help me? I know! Johnny! He's the one who turned Penelope from a proper little madam into a sunnier sort of child. Could he persuade her to give the next governess an easier ride? If he can, I'll jolly well make him a duke.

"Oh bother!" said King Theophilus out loud. "I'd quite forgotten I'd already promised to make the boy a duke and I haven't done anything about it."

The Princess and the under-gardener were weeding the vegetable patch when a footman came to tell Johnny that the King wanted him.

The weeding was quite easy work because Lady Lollipop was rootling along in front of them, loosening the ground and eating such weeds as she fancied, while being very careful (because Johnny had told her to be) not to disturb the rows of plants of cabbage and cauliflower and Brussels sprouts.

"Your dad wants me," Johnny said to the Princess. "Can you manage on your own for a bit? I don't expect I'll be long."

"OK, Duke," said the Princess. "Lollipop's been working hard, I'll give her a break. She likes to go and rootle about in that rough patch down in the corner. I think there must be some tasty weeds there. Are there, Lollipop?"

And the pig grunted "Yes".

"I'm awfully sorry," said the King when Johnny arrived. "I clean forgot I was going to make you a duke. What would you like to be duke of?"

"I'm not that bothered, sir," said Johnny. "I'm quite happy as I am. Was that what you wanted to see me about?"

"Well, no," said the King. "Actually I wanted to have a chat with you about this governess business. Now Miss Gristle has shoved off because of the pig, I've got to find some other woman to replace her."

"The Princess could have a man as a tutor, sir, couldn't she?" said Johnny. "Preferably someone who likes pigs. Mind you, he'd have to be a bit careful."

"What d'you mean?" said the King.

"Well," said Johnny, grinning, "he'd have to mind his p's and q's and not just call her Penelope like Miss Gristle did."

King Theophilus grinned back. "You don't call her 'Your Royal Highness', Johnny, do you?"

"No, sir. But we're friends. Whoever you get, man or woman, Penelope would have to like the person."

"Look, Johnny," said the King, "d'you think you could find me someone? If you could, I'd jolly well make you a prince."

But before Johnny could answer, the

door was flung open and in rushed Princess Penelope.

"Johnny!" she cried. "Come quickly! There's something wrong with Lady Lollipop!" And out she ran again.

"Go on, Johnny," said the King. "Go after her."

In the vegetable patch, Johnny found his pig – Penelope's pig, their pig – lying on her side on top of a squashed row of cabbage plants. Her eyes were closed and she was breathing heavily.

"She went off down to the rough patch," the Princess said, "and after a bit she came back, and then she groaned and collapsed. 'Are you all right?' I asked, and she gave the 'No' grunt. Oh, Duke, whatever's the matter with her?"

Johnny knelt down beside Lollipop. He

spoke to her, asking what the matter was, but she only responded with small squeaks of pain.

"I think she must have a fever of some sort," he said.

"Oh, who could help her?" cried Penelope.

"There's only one person," answered Johnny.

"Who?"

"The Conjuror."

"Conjuror? What does that mean?"

"Well, he's a sort of magician. He's got magic powers, they say, and mostly he uses them to cure sick animals."

"Have you met him, Duke?"

"Yes. He's ever such a funny-looking little man."

"I don't care what he looks like," said Penelope, "as long as he can cure Lollipop. Can you find him?"

"Hope so," said Johnny. "You stay with her

and talk to her. That will comfort you, won't it, Lollipop?" And this time, at the sound of his voice, the pig feebly grunted "Yes".

For hours, it seemed to the Princess, she sat beside her pig, patting her, stroking her, telling her not to worry, everything would be all right, Johnny would find the Conjuror and he would make her better.

The King and the Queen came out into the gardens to see what the matter was, and before long there was a large circle of onlookers standing round the Princess and Lady Lollipop.

As the news spread, the Lord High Chamberlain came out and the Comptroller of the Royal Household and the Master of the Horse and several of the Ladies of the Bedchamber and a whole lot of footmen.

All of them knew how important the pig

was to the happiness of the Princess, and how important the happiness of the Princess was to Their Majesties, and all of them hoped devoutly that Johnny would find the Conjuror.

Then – after ages, it seemed to the Princess, but really after less than an hour – word came that Johnny had been successful in his quest and was on his way, and the King (prompted by the Queen) ordered everyone else to return to their duties.

So that only King Theophilus and Queen Ethelwynne and the Princess Penelope were left to see Johnny Skinner come into the gardens, followed by a very strange figure.

In height, the Conjuror was not much taller than the Princess, so that it seemed as though his beard, which was very long, might trip him up at any moment. He wore strange clothes of many different colours and on his head the oddest sort of tall top hat with no brim.

"May it please Your Majesty," he said to the King in a squeaky voice, "I am Collie Cob, the Conjuror, and I am come to cure Your Majesty's pig."

"It jolly well does please me," said the King, "but she isn't my pig, she's my daughter's. What d'you think is the matter with her?"

The little Conjuror bent his short legs and laid his hands upon the pig's chest, feeling for the beat of her heart. Then he straightened up and addressed Princess Penelope. "Your Royal Highness," he said, "pray what is your pig called?"

"Lady Lollipop," replied the Princess.

"Your Royal Highness," said the Conjuror, "I have to tell you that Lady Lollipop is a very sick pig."

"What's the matter with her?" cried the Princess.

"I think," said the Conjuror, "that she may have eaten some plant or other – deadly nightshade, maybe, or hemlock – that has poisoned her. She has a high fever."

"Oh, please!" cried the Princess. "Can you make her better?"

The Conjuror smiled.

"One thing's certain," he said. "If Collie Cob can't cure her, then nobody can."

# *"I'll jolly well make you a duke"*

"How can we help?" asked the Queen.

"Oh, that is most gracious of Your Majesty," began the Conjuror.

"This is an emergency," said the Queen, "and we need to act fast. You can drop all that 'Majesty' business for now."

At these last words the King looked astonished and Johnny Skinner, catching the Princess's eye, winked at her with one of his own.

"Well," said the Conjuror to the Queen, "I shall need boiling water. Could you put the kettle on?"

"What can I do?" asked the King.

"I shall want a big jug and a large bowl," said Collie Cob, and off went the King and Queen to the Royal kitchens.

"What about us?" asked the Princess and Johnny with one voice.

"You two," said the Conjuror, "can be collecting all that I shall need to make up a potion."

"A magic potion?" asked the Princess.

The Conjuror smiled.

"We shall see," he replied. "Now, here are

the things I shall want. The first and most important, Johnny – and I'm asking you to find it because you're a gardener – is a big bunch of feverfew."

"What's that, Mr Cob?" asked Johnny.

"This is an emergency," said the Conjuror, "and we need to act fast. You can drop all that 'Mr Cob' business for now." And he grinned, his blue eyes twinkling. "Feverfew, Johnny, is a plant of the daisy family, related to camomile and very effective in reducing fever. I just happened to notice a patch of it by the gate we came in through. And while you're about it, get me some spinach leaves and a head of broccoli and a big dandelion. Quick as you can!"

"What about me?" asked Princess Penelope.

"I need two eggs," said the Conjuror. "One brown, one white, and an eggcupful of mustard lightly salted, and the juice of a

lemon. Break the eggs into a bowl and stir the
rest in. Away you go!"

Alone with Lollipop, whose breathing was
still loud and laboured, the Conjuror lifted
one of her big ears and spoke softly into it.
Had anyone heard his words, they would
not have understood them, for they were in a
strange tongue, but the pig's eyelids fluttered
and she gave one tiny grunt that might have
been a "Yes".

Once everyone was back with what the
Conjuror had ordered, he set about
concocting his potion.

Into a large bowl that King Theophilus had
brought, he tipped the mixture that Princess
Penelope had made up. Then he brought
out from a bag that he carried a great pair
of scissors and a wooden ladle. He chopped
very small the dandelion, the broccoli, the

spinach and the big bunch of feverfew that Johnny Skinner had provided, and added them to the mix. Lastly, he took from Queen Ethelwynne the kettle of boiling water and poured it in, and with the wooden ladle he stirred and stirred and stirred the thick green compound.

"Now," he said, "we'll wait for it to cool a bit."

"But how are you going to give it to her?" asked the Princess. "She can't get up, so how will she drink it?"

For answer the Conjuror took from his bag a little funnel and a length of rubber tubing. He fitted them together, slipped the end into Lollipop's mouth and eased it in until he was satisfied that it was down her throat.

Then, after making sure that the mixture was cool enough, he lifted the large bowl (with the King's help, for it was heavy) and between them they tipped it, to pour its contents slowly into the big jug, and thence into the funnel and thus into the tubing and thus into the pig, until the bowl was empty.

Then the Conjuror gently withdrew the length of tubing.

At first it did not seem to the watchers that the potion had had any effect. Still Lady Lollipop lay flat on her side, her eyes closed. Still they heard that harsh painful breathing. Penelope and Johnny both crossed their fingers. The King and Queen held hands tightly.

But then, gradually, to the amazement of the Royal Family and Johnny, the pig's breathing began to quieten. Then her eyelids started to flutter. Then the one eye that they could see slowly opened. Lastly – and loudly – Lady Lollipop let out the most enormous belch.

"She'll be right as rain now," said the

Conjuror. "Come on, Lady Lollipop, up you get!"

And up she got!

"Oh, Lollipop!" cried the Princess. "Are you all right, my dear?"

At which the pig gave a loud and definite "Yes" grunt, shook herself and looked around with bright eyes at each person in turn. She looked particularly gratefully at the short figure of Collie Cob, the Conjuror, whose hand the King was now heartily shaking.

"Marvellous!" said King Theophilus. "You're a wizard, Mr Cob! I'll jolly well make you a duke!"

Johnny Skinner spoke softly in the Conjuror's ear.

"I shouldn't rely on it, if I were you," he said.

# "Bird droppings and slug slime and mashed mouse manure"

"Well, anyway," said the King, "you must let us pay you for your services. You have saved Lollipop's life. What do we owe you?"

"Oh, bless you, sir, that's all right," said the Conjuror. "I'm glad to have been of service.

To have lost such a fine young pig would have been a tragedy. She's going to grow into a beautiful sow. I can just see her with a litter of lovely little piglets."

At this the King smiled broadly, Johnny grinned with delight, and the Princess Penelope jumped up and down in excitement. Even the pig let out a string of quick high-pitched grunts to show her pleasure at the Conjuror's forecast.

Only the Queen looked doubtful. Fond as she was by now of her daughter's pet, she recoiled at the thought of nine or ten miniature Lollipops scampering around in the Palace.

She picked up the kettle.

"Come and have a cup of tea," she said, and off she marched, the Conjuror following.

The King picked up the big jug and the large bowl and the smaller bowl in which Penelope had brought the mixture for the potion.

"Coming?" he said to the two children.

"No, Daddy," said the Princess. "I'm going to stay with Lollipop. You go if you want, Johnny."

"No," said Johnny, "I'll stay with you."

Once King and Queen and Conjuror were all seated round the Royal dining-table drinking tea, King Theophilus tried once more to offer payment for the treatment of the pig, but the Conjuror was adamant.

"No, sir," he said, "thanking you kindly. I treat all kinds of animals for all kinds of people but I never charge for my services, for most of those who seek my help are poor folk."

"We're not," said the Queen.

"No, ma'am, but I never take money from anyone. The most I accept, from those that can afford it, is payment in kind – a couple of pounds of potatoes perhaps or a bundle of firewood or a dozen eggs."

"How are we to thank you then?" asked the Queen.

What a strange little man he is, she thought, with his squeaky voice and his many-coloured clothes and his funny hat.

"Well, ma'am," said the Conjuror, "there is one favour that Your Majesties could grant me, and that is to let me come back now and again, to see that Lollipop is all right and to meet again with your daughter and the boy Johnny and to admire once more that beautiful garden of roses – my favourite flowers – that we passed just now."

What a lovely little man he is, thought the Queen.

"How do you grow such wonderful blooms, may I ask?" said the Conjuror. "What is the secret of your success?"

"Pig dung," said the Queen.

"First class!" squeaked the Conjuror.

"Some rose-growers prefer horse dung, but I think pig is the best. Whilst we're on the subject, I notice that your bushes suffer from that scourge of rose-growers – black spot."

"They do, they do," said the Queen. "I don't know what to do about it and nor does Johnny. It worries us no end."

"Worry no more," said the Conjuror.

"Why? Can you cure it?"

"I can, ma'am. If you will allow me I will treat the affected leaves with a special dressing of my own invention, a mixture of bird droppings and slug slime and mashed mouse manure."

"Then by all means," cried the Queen, "come back to my rose-garden as soon as you can, Mr Cob, and come as often as you can to visit us and the children!"

"And the pig," added the King.

*What a clever little chap he is*, he thought.

"What a knowledgeable fellow you are, to

be sure," he said. "First you cure the pig and now you're going to put my wife's roses to rights. What favour, I wonder, will you do us next?"

"It depends, sir," said the Conjuror. "Has Your Majesty any other problem at the present time?"

"Yes!" said the King. "Come to think of it, I jolly well have. We need a governess." And he told the Conjuror all about the newly departed Miss Gristle.

"You don't know of any woman suitable for the job, I suppose?" he asked.

For a moment the little Conjuror did not answer but looked reflectively at King Theophilus and Queen Ethelwynne.

What a nice couple they are, he thought. I dare say I could teach the two children quite a lot. It'd be fun to try.

"Does it have to be a woman?" he asked.

Funny, thought the King, that's just what Johnny said.

"No," he replied, "it could be a man. We need someone to teach the Princess reading and writing and arithmetic and all that sort of stuff."

"And to teach the boy too," said the Queen.

"And the pig," said the King. "She's pretty bright."

"Then, sir," said the Conjuror, "I think I know of a man who would like to try his hand at that job."

"You do?" cried the King and Queen together.

"Yes."

"Who?" they said.

"Me," replied Collie Cob, the Conjuror.

"When can you start?" they cried.

# *"How would you like to be Penny?"*

In fact it was a week before the new tutor entered the schoolroom.

First, there were several sick animals that the Conjuror had to treat – a horse with the staggers, a cow with bloat, some sheep with swayback and a goat with garget – and, secondly, he needed to make up that mixture of bird droppings and slug slime and mashed mouse manure, to rid the Queen's roses of black spot.

But at last the day came when the Conjuror and the Princess and Johnny Skinner and Lady Lollipop all met within the Palace schoolroom.

The Princess Penelope was the first to speak.

"Please," she said, "what are we to call you?"

"Well," said the Conjuror, "my name, as you know, is Collie Cob. You could call me Mr Cob, I suppose, but that doesn't sound friendly enough to me, so why don't you just call me 'Collie'?"

Johnny grinned and the pig gave a grunt that definitely meant "I agree" and Penelope said, "OK, Collie. Thanks."

"And what, pray," said the Conjuror, "would you like me to call you?"

The Princess smiled.

"Just Penelope," she said.

"Very well," said the Conjuror. "Though I've just had a thought. There's a sort of plant that I often use in making my potions. It's a kind of mint and its name is pennyroyal. You're royal, so how would you like to be Penny?"

"Suits me, Collie."

"Now then," said the Conjuror, "this morning we're going to think about numbers. Tell me, Penny, how many of us are there in this schoolroom?"

"Four," said the Princess.

"How many humans, Johnny?"

"Three."

"How many females, Penny?"

"Two."

"How many grown-ups, Johnny?"

"One."

The Conjuror turned to Lady Lollipop.

"How many pigs?" he asked her, and the answer was one sharp grunt.

"I don't know what you two think," said Collie Cob, "but I don't much like this old schoolroom, specially when the sun is shining. How about doing lessons outside?"

"Great!" said Penelope and Johnny and "Grunt!" said Lollipop.

So they all three went out into the garden with the Conjuror.

How can he teach us out here, the children were thinking, without all that stuff Miss Gristle had in the schoolroom?

But then Collie said, "Right. Off we go!"

"Where are we going?" they asked.

"For a walk."

"Where to?"

"Round the town."

"Why?"

"We're going to do some reading," Collie said. "There'll be signs to read, wherever we go, and I can teach you what they say."

And sure enough, even while they were still in the Palace grounds, they came across lots of notices saying, KEEP OFF THE GRASS and PRIVATE NO ENTRY and TRESPASSERS WILL BE PROSECUTED.

And once they were in the town, there were things to read everywhere: the names of streets, the names of shopkeepers, and the names of things for sale in the shops, like, for instance, in the greengrocer's – APPLES, ORANGES, BANANAS, TOMATOES, CABBAGES, CARROTS, on and on.

And there were lots of numbers too – the numbers on price-tags, the numbers of houses – so that by the end of that first morning, Penelope and Johnny had done a lot of work with words and figures.

As for Lady Lollipop, she had had a lovely time in the greengrocer's, for the shopkeeper was only too eager to offer the Princess's pet pig a lot of lovely fruit and vegetables.

## CHAPTER SEVEN

# *"The facts I'm going to learn today"*

Never was there such a tutor as Collie Cob,
the Conjuror. Admittedly he was teaching
two very keen pupils – Johnny Skinner,
revelling in learning how to read and to write,
and the Princess, quick and bright, who was

learning to enjoy reading stories and indeed
to begin writing some of her own making, in
a clear bold hand.

The pair of them were not being taught
every day, for the Conjuror was sometimes
called upon to treat a sick animal, but
then they did not need as many lessons as
ordinary children would have done, because
most of the many things the Conjuror taught
them seemed to stick.

Once told a fact, they seldom forgot it.

"It's magic, Duke, isn't it?" said the Princess
to her friend after they'd been having lessons
for a couple of weeks.

"It must be, Penny," Johnny replied (he had
taken to calling her that too now). "It's all to
do with that little rhyme that Collie taught us."

For before a day's lessons – whether
in reading or writing or maths or history
or geography or science – the Princess and

Johnny would solemnly chant together:

> "The facts I'm going to learn today
> Will have a job to go away.
> Most will remain inside my brain.
> I shan't need to be told again."

And the magic worked!

The King and Queen were amazed at the things the children knew, which they didn't.

The Princess Penelope specially enjoyed examining her parents.

"Daddy," she said to the King. "Do you know the date of the spring equinox?"

"Er, no," said King Theophilus. (What's an equinox? he thought.)

"Twenty-first of March," said his daughter. "And the autumn equinox?"

"Um, er, twenty-first of September?" said the King.

"No, Daddy, no, it's the twenty-third of September."

"I should have thought you'd have known that, Theo," said the Queen sniffily.

"You did, Mummy, did you?" Penelope asked.

"Any fool would know that," replied Queen Ethelwynne.

"In that case, Mummy," said Penelope, "you obviously know what an equinox is?"

The Queen hesitated.

"Oh come on, Eth," said the King. "Any fool would know that."

"An equinox," said the Princess Penelope, "is either of the two points at which the ecliptic intersects the celestial equator. OK, Mummy? OK, Daddy?"

As for Johnny Skinner, Collie Cob, realizing the boy's interest in gardening, slipped in some lessons in botany and biology, which resulted, amongst other things, in great improvements to the Queen's roses (free now of black spot) and made Her Majesty even more delighted with her under-gardener.

So the weeks and months passed, and the Conjuror's two pupils gained more and more knowledge of more and more things.

As for Lollipop, she seemed to grow wiser and wiser.

One day when the children were playing and the pig and her tutor were resting on the Royal grass (not keeping off it at all), the Conjuror said to her, in her own language, "You're a clever girl, Lollipop, aren't you?"

In answer there came a very loud "Yes" grunt.

## CHAPTER EIGHT

# "A moly is a magic herb"

Of course, there are lots of things that humans can do which pigs can't.

But, apart from being a very intelligent pig, Lollipop had two advantages over the children, over the King and Queen, even over

Collie Cob. She had a very acute sense of smell, and she had a snout specially designed for rootling in the ground.

By chance the day came when she needed both these gifts.

For some time King Theophilus had been worried about his increasing weight, for he had become a great deal more tubby.

One day the Queen had said to him, "Honestly, Theo, you're getting as fat as a pig!"

The remark was light-hearted, but the more the King thought about it, the more he became determined to go on a diet.

At breakfast, his usual ration of two helpings of scrambled eggs on fried bread became one helping only.

Then he told them not to bother with the fried bread.

Then he said he'd just have one boiled egg.

By rights he should have become hungrier

as he ate less. But instead, the less he ate, the less hungry he felt. At last one morning – and this worried the Queen greatly – he said he didn't feel like any breakfast at all, but just sat at the table, looking pale (and much thinner).

Queen Ethelwynne called in all sorts of different doctors, who examined the King and scratched their heads and finally confessed that they did not have a clue how to restore the King's appetite.

Leaving her husband sitting gloomily at the breakfast table, the Queen went out into the garden and there found Johnny Skinner hard at work, though it was drizzling with rain.

"Oh, Johnny!" she cried. "His Majesty is most unwell and none of the doctors know why. If he doesn't start to eat properly again soon, he'll just fade away. What shall I do?"

Just then Princess Penelope stuck her head out of the schoolroom window. "Johnny!"

she shouted. "Collie says lessons in here this morning because of the rain."

"Coming!" called Johnny. And to the Queen he said, "It sounds to me, Your Majesty, as though the King needs a touch of magic to make him better."

"Magic?" said the Queen. "You mean...?" And she pointed up to the schoolroom window.

Johnny nodded.

Lessons that morning consisted of reading, because Collie Cob, the Conjuror, was called away by the Queen to examine the King, leaving the Princess with her nose in a book about astronomy (on which she was very keen), and Johnny with his nose in a book entitled *The Values of Various Kinds of Manure in Garden Fertilization* (something that interested him greatly).

Lollipop snoozed in an armchair.

Both the children shut their books with a snap when the Conjuror came back into the schoolroom.

"Oh, Collie!" cried Penelope. "Whatever's the matter with Daddy, do you know?"

"He's lost his appetite," said the Conjuror. He patted Lollipop's head. "That's something pigs don't usually do," he said, smiling.

"Can you cure him?" the children said.

"With a little help from someone," he replied. "Now then, Penny and Johnny, you've read long enough. Time you had a break. Off you go and play."

When they had gone, the Conjuror called Lollipop out of her chair and invited her to sit in front of the blackboard. Then he took a piece of chalk and drew upon it what seemed to be a picture of a plant of some kind, an odd-looking plant with a feathery top and – below a line which he drew across the board – a strange bulbous root, not round or oval like a potato, for example, but long and curved, the shape of a banana.

Then he began to speak to Lollipop in pig language, a curious mixture of snuffles and snorts and squeaks.

"Now see these leaves," he said to her, pointing above the chalk line on the blackboard, "and this root" – pointing below. "This, Lollipop, is a picture of a moly. A moly is a magic herb, a species of wild onion, and I am going to take you out in the woods to see if you can find one for me. I cannot show you exactly what it smells like because I haven't got one to show you. But if you can rootle up anything that smells oniony and you find that its root is shaped like a banana, then that's a moly. And only a moly can cure the King."

That afternoon Collie Cob asked the children if they would like a walk in the woods.

"It's a lovely day," he said to them, "and Lady Lollipop will enjoy a bit of exercise. Who knows, she might find something exciting."

"What d'you mean?" asked the Princess.

"Like what?" asked Johnny.

"Oh, I don't know," said the Conjuror, dressed, as always, in his curious many-coloured clothes and wearing his tall brimless top hat.

He smiled.

"Pigs are good at finding things. You never can tell what she might turn up."

Once in the woods the two children, at the Conjuror's suggestion, ran off among the trees to play hide-and-seek.

"It's the same game for you, Lollipop," the

Conjuror said. "The moly's hiding and you're seeking. Does this feel like a good sort of place to you?" And the pig gave the "Yes" grunt.

For quite a while she snuffled around, occasionally rootling up plants with her snout, but not finding what she'd been told to find.

Collie was about to lead her on to a different part of the woods when suddenly he heard Lollipop give a loud excited squeal as she came across an odd-looking plant with a feathery top.

Quickly she dug around it with her strong (and by now very dirty) snout, and hoicked it up out of the ground, root and all, a root that was the shape of a banana.

She picked up the whole plant and laid it carefully at the feet of the Conjuror.

"You," said he, "are a very clever pig," and he called loudly, "Penny! Johnny!" and when they came running, he picked up the plant and waved it at them.

"Whatever's that?" asked the Princess.

And Johnny, the gardener, said, "What a strange-looking root it's got. What is it?"

"This," said Collie Cob, "is a magic plant called a moly, which clever Lollipop has found for us. From its root I can make a preparation that will restore the appetite of someone who's lost his."

"Dad!" cried Princess Penelope.

The Conjuror nodded.

"Come on," he said. "We must hurry back to the Palace. There's no time to be lost, for only a moly can save your father's life."

## CHAPTER NINE

# "Anything to stop you all nagging me"

The four of them made their way out of
the woods, the Conjuror carrying the moly,
Penny and Johnny on either side of him,
Lollipop bringing up the rear and stopping
every now and again to rootle up something

that looked to her good to eat and then galloping after them to catch up.

"Daddy hasn't got to eat all of that funny root, has he?" the Princess asked.

"No, he hasn't," replied Collie. "He wouldn't anyway because he's lost his appetite for any sort of food. But he still has to drink – everybody must have liquid to stay alive."

"So you're going to make the moly into a drink, are you?" Johnny asked.

"Yes," said the Conjuror. "When I get it home, I'll chop the root up small and pound the bits into a nice squishy mess, and then boil them. Then I'll drain off all the liquid – magic liquid – and give it to the King to drink."

Later that day, when the Conjuror came back to the Palace, the children and the pig could see that he was carrying a flask full of a thin golden fluid.

"This is the stuff," he said to the Princess, "to bring your father's appetite back."

"Can I have a swig of it first?" Penelope said.

"No!" said Collie Cob. "You certainly cannot, you stupid girl."

These words turned Princess Penelope back into the spoiled child she had once been. She stamped her foot and shouted at the Conjuror, "How dare you call me a stupid girl! Have you forgotten that I am a princess?"

Behind her back Johnny Skinner put a hand over his mouth to hide a broad grin.

"No, I have not forgotten," said Collie Cob, "and kindly don't shout at me like that, Penny. I can tell you that if you were to drink some of this stuff, it would give you such a raging appetite that you'd eat and eat until you blew up like a balloon. You'd end up the fattest princess in the whole wide world."

"And we don't want that, do we, Lollipop?"

said Johnny, and the pig gave a loud "No" grunt.

"Come on," said the Conjuror. "We'll all go and watch the King take his medicine."

They found King Theophilus sitting once more at the big table in the grand banqueting-hall, where Queen Ethelwynne was trying to tempt him with a number of savoury dishes.

"Try a little of this, Theo," she was saying. "Just a little, to please me. Or some of this ... or this ... or a taste of this."

But the King only said sadly, "I'm not hungry, Eth. I don't want anything to eat."

The Conjuror came forward, flask in one hand, a glass in the other.

"Excuse me," he said to the pale-faced King, "but I have a drink here which I think Your Majesty might find refreshing."

He filled the glass with the thin golden fluid.

"Can I persuade you to try a little sip?" he said.

"No," said the King.

"Oh do, Theo, please!" cried the Queen.

"Please drink it, Daddy," cried the Princess.

"It'll do you good, sir," said Johnny.

The Conjuror held out the glass.

"Just try it," he said.

"Oh, all right, if I must," growled the King. "Anything to stop you all nagging me."

And he took the glass and looked at it and sniffed it, while Lollipop gave a little volley of "Yes" grunts.

Then he took a sip of the magic draught made from the moly.

Immediately, they could all see, his dull eyes brightened and a little colour came back into his grey cheeks.

Then he took several big gulps.

Then he drained the glass.

As they all watched, King Theophilus rose to his feet, looking around him somewhat dazedly, as though waking from a bad dream.

Then he shouted at the top of his voice, "Breakfast! I want my breakfast!"

"But Theo," said Queen Ethelwynne, "it's teatime."

"He wants to break his fast," said the Conjuror quietly to the Queen.

So she said to her husband, "What would you like?"

"Scrambled eggs!" the King shouted. "A double helping of scrambled eggs! With three rounds of fried bread! And be quick about it, I'm starving!"

Back in the schoolroom, the Princess said to the Conjuror, "Thank you, Collie. Thank you so much for bringing Daddy's appetite back – for saving his life in fact. And I'm sorry I shouted at you. It was very rude of me."

"Good for you," said Johnny under his breath.

"That's all right, Penny," said the Conjuror. "Anyway, I couldn't have cured your father without the magic moly and I couldn't have found that without Lollipop's help. Now then, why don't you both go and see how the King's getting on with his meal?"

In fact, when they reached the banqueting-hall, the King was on his third helping of scrambled eggs and his fourth bit of fried bread, and waiting on the table beside him was another of his favourite dishes: cold rice pudding with lashings of strawberry jam.

Left alone with Lollipop, Collie Cob had a word in her great ear.

"I rather think," he said, "that King Theophilus is making a pig of himself."

ᴏ჻ —— CHAPTER TEN —— ჻ᴏ

## *"Good old Lady Lollipop"*

Thanks to the moly, a whole lot of things

now changed for King Theophilus.

First, of course, his appetite was restored,

and how! Happily he ate, all day long, and

as a result put on so much weight that

Queen Ethelwynne decided he must take some exercise.

"Go for a walk," she said.

"By myself?" said the King.

"Well, I've got too much to do in the Palace and in the gardens, and Penelope and Johnny have their lessons with the Conjuror."

"The pig's not doing anything," said the King.

"All right then, take her with you on your walks. Exercise won't do her any harm."

So the second new thing that happened was that every morning, once he had digested a very big breakfast, the King would set out from the Palace with Lady Lollipop beside him. She did not need a collar and lead as a dog would have done, but walked to heel at the King's side and did everything he told her, like "Stop!" (when he wanted to talk to a passer-by) or "Sit!" (when he needed a breather).

The third thing that happened was that the King found himself becoming extremely fond of his daughter's pet. He remembered how small and skinny she had been when first they'd set eyes on her. Now she was a fine strong pig. She was good company on his walks and he talked to her a good deal as they went along, telling her what a good and beautiful pig she was, and how grateful to her he was for finding (as the Conjuror had told him) the moly.

"I'd like to do something for you in return," said the King. "Is there something you specially want?" And in reply Lollipop let out a fusillade of excited noises (which of course meant nothing to the King).

One day he said to the Conjuror, "Look here, Cob, I'd very much like your advice. I think you know that I take Lollipop for

regular walks now – my wife's got a bee
in her bonnet about me needing exercise –
and the pig talks to me a good deal, but of
course I can't understand pig language." King
Theophilus laughed heartily. "Just imagine, if
one could!" he said.

"Just imagine," said the Conjuror.

"You see," said the King, "I'm curious to
know what the animal wants, because I'm
fairly sure there's something on her mind. You
couldn't help, I suppose, Cob, could you?"

"It's possible," said the Conjuror. "I'll have
a word with her."

"Have a word with her!" laughed the King.
"You'd have to speak her own language to
do that!"

"Just so," said the Conjuror.

"Anyway," said the King, "see if you can
work out what it is that Lollipop wants.
I'd like to do something for her. Fancy her

finding that ... what's it called?"

"Moly."

"Yes, that's it. Good old Lady Lollipop! I'll jolly well make her a duchess," said the King.

Next morning, a lovely sunny morning, they were having lessons in the garden.

"Your father," said Collie Cob to the Princess, "says he's going to make Lady Lollipop a duchess."

"Pigs might fly!" said the Princess scornfully. "Daddy's always saying things like that."

She turned to Johnny.

"Isn't he, Duke?" she said.

Johnny smiled.

"Don't get excited," she said to the Conjuror, "if he offers to make you Sir Collie Cob. He always forgets."

"Well," said the Conjuror, "luckily you two will never forget any of the things that I have taught you. Like, for instance, Gondwanaland. What was Gondwanaland, Penny?"

"A supercontinent," replied the Princess, "which is believed to have existed more than two hundred million years ago. It probably consisted of South America, Africa, Australia, Antarctica and India."

"Quite right," said the Conjuror. "Now, one for you, Johnny. What is a numbat?"

"It's a rat-sized marsupial," said Johnny, "with white stripes across its back and a long tail, and it feeds on ants and termites with its sticky tongue."

"And how are numbats different from all other marsupials?" Collie asked.

"They don't have a pouch."

"Good," said the Conjuror. "And here's one for both of you. How far is Earth from the sun?"

And with one voice they replied, "Ninety-three million miles!"

"Right," said the Conjuror. "Have a break now. Run to the bottom of the garden and back." And as they dashed off, he said to Lady Lollipop, "Stay here with me a minute."

He looked into those bright eyes, fringed with long white lashes and filled with intelligence, and saw someone not so very different from himself looking back at him.

The pig in her turn looked up at the funny little man dressed in many-coloured clothes and wearing that odd brimless top hat, and made the kind of noise that meant, "What's up, then?"

"Now then, Lollipop," said the Conjuror, "the King tells me that he thinks there's something on your mind. Nothing wrong with you, is there? You're not feeling ill again?"

In reply came that deep long-drawn-out "No" grunt.

"Well, what is it that you want?"

The children arrived back from their race – Johnny won, he had longer legs – in time to hear Lollipop's answer, a babble of grunts and squeaks and snorts and snuffles.

"She's trying to tell us something," said the Princess. "I wish I knew what she wants."

"I think I can guess," said Johnny. "My Lollipop" – he turned to smile at Penny – "*our* Lollipop, is a healthy young female, nearly full-grown now."

Johnny Skinner and Penelope looked at Collie Cob and then they looked at one another.

"Of course!" they said with one voice. "She wants babies!"

## CHAPTER ELEVEN

## *"Dark and handsome"*

The Conjuror thought carefully about what the pig wanted. The Princess would be delighted at the idea and so would Johnny, and the King too, now that he'd become so fond of Lollipop. The Queen, though, she might not be all that keen.

Well, said Collie Cob to himself, we must make some changes.

"Penny," he said to the Princess, "does Lollipop still sleep on your bed?"

"Yes."

"Plenty of room for her, is there?"

"Well..."

"Still get up the stairs quite easily, can she?"

"Well..."

"She doesn't disturb you at nights, by snoring or making any other noises?"

"Well, she..."

"Don't you think," said the Conjuror, "that it's time she had a room of her own?"

"A bedroom, you mean?"

"Yes. Downstairs. Close to the pig-flap."

"That reminds me," said the Princess. "She's getting too big for that pig-flap. The other day she got stuck in it and Johnny and I had to get a footman to help us push her through."

"That's no problem," said the Conjuror. "We'll get the Royal carpenters to make a larger one. Now then, about a room for her – there's that nice one right next to the schoolroom. It doesn't seem to be used for anything much."

"I'll ask Mummy if I can have it for Lollipop," the Princess said.

"Good," said the Conjuror. "Or perhaps, better still, tell Mummy you want it for Lollipop."

In fact Queen Ethelwynne was quite pleased with the idea. Fond as she had become of Lollipop because of all the good she did in the rose-garden, cultivating the soil with her snout and manuring it at the other end, she had never been all that keen on the pig walking over her priceless carpets or up the stairs, nor on her sleeping in Penelope's bedroom.

So she gave orders for the nice room next door to the schoolroom to be cleared of its furniture and (at the Princess's suggestion) for its carpet to be covered in a good thick layer of horse-blankets from the Royal Mews, to make a really comfortable bed.

Not until Lollipop was settled into her new quarters and a new, much larger, pig-flap had been fitted, did the Conjuror take King Theophilus into his confidence.

"You remember," he said to the King, "you wanted me to find out what was on the pig's mind?"

No, thought the King.

"Yes," he said.

"Well, we've found out what she wants!" cried Johnny and the Princess together.

"What does she want then?"

"Babies."

"Babies!" cried the King. "Oh I say, what fun, Cob!"

"What about your wife, sir?"

"Well, we needn't say anything to her, need we? Let's make it a surprise."

"If you like."

"Can you fix it, Cob?" said the King. "Can you arrange it all? I mean, do you know someone who keeps a … what do you call a … father pig?"

"A boar."

"Yes, that's it."

"Yes, I do."

"If you can fix it," said the King excitedly, "I'll jolly well make you a knight! Sir Collie Cob! How does that sound?"

Awful, thought the Conjuror.

"Very nice," he said.

Now amongst all the many things that the Conjuror knew was the fact that it takes a sow three months, three weeks and three days to have babies.

In the schoolroom he steered the conversation round to birthdays.

"When's yours, Johnny?" he asked.

"December the ninth," said Johnny.

"And yours, Penny?"

"June the twenty-third."

Quickly the Conjuror did a sum in his head. It might work out just right, he thought. It's the middle of February now, so if I take Lollipop to the boar towards the end of the month, then the piglets might be born round about Penny's birthday. *On* Penny's birthday, he said to himself. With a bit of luck. Or magic.

"When's yours, Collie?" the Princess asked.

"April the first."

So, nearly two weeks later, it was not King Theophilus who took Lady Lollipop for her daily walk. It was Collie Cob. He had told her, of course, what he had planned for her and asked her if she thought it was a good idea, and she had replied that it was a very good idea indeed, and, in a salvo of excited snorts and snuffles, asked, "What's he like, this boar?"

"Dark and handsome," said the Conjuror.

∘⊰ ───── CHAPTER TWELVE ───── ⊱∘
## "Oh, Collie, you fixed it!"

If you're eagerly waiting for something to
happen, time can pass very slowly.

Not only the King but also Johnny Skinner
(who had been told but sworn to secrecy)
knew that Lollipop was, in due course, to

become a mother. But that due course – of three months, three weeks and three days – seemed an awful long time.

Lollipop didn't seem worried by the wait. She enjoyed her food and her daily exercise with the King, and slept like a log in her new bedroom, from which, when she needed to, it was easy to pop out into the garden through the new very large pig-flap.

For the Queen and the Princess Penelope, time passed at its usual rate for neither was expecting anything unusual to happen. The Queen was happy in her garden and Penelope was happy having lessons with the Conjuror and being taught so many interesting facts, none of which, once learned, was ever forgotten.

She still rather liked to show off her new-found knowledge to her parents.

"Mummy," she might say to the Queen,

"do you know what is the official language of India?"

"Indian, I suppose," replied her mother.

"No, it's Hindi."

"Oh," said the Queen.

Or, "Daddy," she might say to the King, "d'you know what a moa is?"

"Thing you cut the lawn with," said the King.

"No, not M–O–W–E–R. M–O–A."

"Oh. No. Haven't a clue."

"It's an extinct flightless bird that used to live in New Zealand. It had a little head and a long neck and it could run very fast."

"Proper clever clogs you are," said the King one day. "But I bet I know something that you don't."

"What?"

"Can't tell you. It's a secret."

"Oh go on, Daddy!"

"You'll find out before you're much older," said the King.

"It's my birthday soon," said his daughter. "Just in case you forget. Has this secret got anything to do with that?"

The King winked at her, but he wouldn't say another word.

The Princess consulted Johnny.

"Duke," she said. "Daddy's on about some secret, something to do with my birthday, I think. D'you know anything about it?"

"Yes."

"What is it?"

"It's a secret."

The Princess's face darkened and she frowned furiously and stamped her foot, which made Johnny smile, remembering what she used to be like.

"What are you grinning at, Duke?"

she said angrily.

"Patience, Penny," said Johnny.

"Patience is a virtue,
Virtue is a grace,
Grace is a little girl
Who wouldn't wash her face."

Before she went to bed that night, the
Princess went into Lollipop's new quarters
to give her her supper. She stood watching as
the pig golloped down a great deal of food.

"You're certainly very hungry these days,
Lady Lollipop," she said, "and you seem to be
getting fatter too." In reply the pig made a lot
of loud snorty snuffly squeaky noises.

"I wish I could understand what you're
saying," sighed the Princess. "Still, you look
pretty happy. Are you happy?" And in reply
came half a dozen loud clear "Yes" grunts.

Of course, Lady Lollipop's original owner
knew why she was eating so heartily and
why she had apparently put on so much
weight. Johnny Skinner was delighted and
excited to think that, before long, his pig ...
Penny's pig ... their pig, would give birth to
a litter of piglets.

And how many would she have, he
wondered. He knew that sometimes pigs can
have as many as twelve or even more babies
at one birth, but he knew also that a young
sow like Lollipop would not have so many in
her first litter.

And what colour would they be, he
thought. He knew – because the Conjuror
had told the King, who had told him – that
the father of those unborn piglets was a very
handsome coal-black boar.

Halfway through the month of June, Johnny was getting rather impatient for the answers to his questions.

King Theophilus also was very excited. How marvellous it would be if the pig actually had her babies on Penelope's birthday! What a wonderful day that would make it for the Princess! Nothing must spoil it, he thought. Then he suddenly thought that there was one person who might spoil it and that was his wife, who knew nothing of the secret and might object very strongly to the Palace being full of pigs.

I'll see if Cob can fix it, he said to himself. Eth thinks the world of that fellow since he cured her roses of black spot with that mixture of bird droppings and slug slime and mashed mouse manure.

"Don't worry yourself," the Conjuror

said to the King. "I will have a word with Her Majesty, pointing out that Lollipop and however many babies she may have will be downstairs and close to the pig-flap and thus to the rose-garden, where in due course Queen Ethelwynne will have not just one pig to cultivate and manure her rose-beds, but lots."

"She's sure to be niggled," said the King, "because – apart from Penelope – she's the last to be told the secret."

"With your permission, sir," said the Conjuror, "I shall tell a little white lie. I shall tell the Queen that she is the first to be told. That ought to please her."

So he did, and it did!

On the evening of June the twenty-second, the Queen's under-gardener went to sleep in his little cottage, hoping very much that Lollipop would give birth the following day.

Johnny had been to say good night to her in her room and had seen that she was restless, moving the layers of horse-blankets about with her snout, as though trying to make some sort of bed.

He woke early next morning and dressed and crossed the garden. He ducked in through the new big pig-flap and stood in the passage outside Lollipop's room and listened.

To his great delight Johnny could hear a lot of little grunts and squeaks.

"Oh, Collie, you fixed it!" he said softly.

"No, no," said a voice behind him, and there stood the Conjuror in his many-coloured clothes. In his hand was his tall brimless top hat, which he'd taken off to get through the pig-flap. He put it back on his head.

"No," he said again. "It was nothing to do with me, Johnny, how could it have been? Lady Lollipop just decided that she would

have her babies on Penny's ninth birthday.
A pure coincidence."

Johnny grinned.

"Wait till she sees them!" he said.

In fact they did not have to wait long, for
in a few moments the Princess came running
down the stairs and along the passage.

"Happy birthday, Penny!" said Johnny and
the Conjuror with one voice.

"Oh, thank you!" said the Princess. "I'm
just going to say good morning to my pig."

"*Our* pig," said Johnny.

Your pigs, thought the Conjuror.

At that instant, the Princess also heard the
chorus of noise in Lollipop's room.

She dashed in. There, on a great nest of
horse-blankets, lay Lady Lollipop, nursing
her newborn piglets.

"Oh, how wonderful!" cried Princess
Penelope. "Oh, Lollipop, how clever you

are! Oh, what beautiful babies – some black, some white, some spotty! Oh, Johnny! Oh, Collie!"

The Princess lost no time in telling the news to her parents, and soon King Theophilus and Queen Ethelwynne arrived in their dressing-gowns, the King's nightcap still on his head.

"Oh, Lollipop!" cried the Queen. "What a clever girl you are!"

She turned to her husband.

"I was the first to be told the secret," she said. "You didn't know, Theo, did you?"

"Of course not, Eth," said the King.

He turned to his daughter.

"How many babies has she?" he asked.

"Well, Daddy," replied the Princess, "she has three white ones, two black ones and four spotty ones, and you know what three plus two plus four make, don't you?"

"Of course," said the King. "Um, er, let me see..."

"Nine!" cried the Princess.

o⸄ ── **CHAPTER THIRTEEN** ── ᵹo

## *"What a lovely surprise!"*

When the grown-ups had gone, the King and
Queen to get dressed for breakfast (to which
they had invited the Conjuror), Princess
Penelope and Johnny Skinner stood side by
side, watching Lollipop suckling her babies.

"Oh, Duke," said the Princess. "What a lovely surprise! To think – I never knew! And she's had them on my birthday! And she's had nine, one for each year of my life! However did it happen?"

"Magic, I dare say," replied Johnny. "Mind you, she's clever, your pig is."

"*Our* pig," said the Princess. "Just think, we've got ten pigs now, Duke."

She looked at her friend.

"Daddy still hasn't remembered to make you one," she said.

"Doesn't worry me, Penny," said Johnny. "I'm quite happy just for you to call me that. By the way, the Conjuror told me that your father said he'd make him Sir Collie Cob."

"He'll forget," said the Princess. "Anyway, I think Lollipop's the one who really deserves to be honoured. No good asking Daddy. We'll do it, you and me. What shall we call her?"

Johnny looked fondly at the pig that had once been his and now was theirs, that had once been skinny and now was beautifully plump.

"She doesn't need another title," he said. "Let's just call her Clever Lollipop!"

**Dick King-Smith (1922–2011)** is one of the world's best loved children's book authors. He won the Guardian Children's Fiction Prize for *The Sheep-Pig* (filmed as *Babe*), was named Children's Book Author of the Year in 1991 and received the 1995 Children's Book Award for *Harriet's Hare*. His fiction titles for Walker include the much-loved Sophie series, *The Finger-Eater*, *Aristotle*, *The Twin Giants* and *My Animal Friends*. For more information, visit:
**www.dickkingsmith.com**

**Anna Chernyshova** graduated from Cambridge School of Art's MA in Children's Book Illustration in 2015. She mostly works digitally and enjoys experimenting with different media and textures. She lives in Cambridge with her family, and she can often be found searching for nature and wildlife with her trusty sketchbook. Her mischievous young daughter and the family dog constantly inspire her illustrations and storytelling. For more information, visit:
**www.cherypic.com**